Gallows Bound

Against the odds, having hunted down and cornered the notorious outlaw Frank Cuskin, Marshal Abe Ryan realizes that his problems are only just beginning. Lack of sleep, the desert, Indians, Cuskin's polecat kin, thirst and exhaustion are a combination which, on the long ride ahead, make it ever more likely that Ryan's mission will end in failure.

When Cuskin gets the upper hand and leaves him for dead, a lesser man than Abe Ryan would have abandoned the task and traded the dangers of his mission for his previous easy life as town marshal. But Ryan is not a lesser man, and he will use every weapon in his arsenal to deliver the killer to the gallows.

Gallows Bound

Ben Coady

A Black Horse Western

ROBERT HALE · LONDON

© James O'Brien 2012
First published in Great Britain 2012

ISBN 978-0-7090-9597-2

Robert Hale Limited
Clerkenwell House
Clerkenwell Green
London EC1R 0HT

www.halebooks.com

Typeset by
Derek Doyle & Associates, Shaw Heath
Printed and bound in Great Britain by
CPI Antony Rowe, Chippenham and Eastbourne

*In Fond Memory of Jerry O'Brien
(1936–2011)*

CHAPTER ONE

Marshal Abe Ryan looked out from the ridge across the seemingly endless desert landscape; barren inhospitable terrain that had a thousand and more ways to ensnare a man and send him to hell or heaven, depending on how good or evil his years had been, in the throes of a terrible death. It was only an hour after sunrise, but already the vastness was enshrouded in a shimmer of heat that was as deceptive as a two-timing woman's heart. What seemed benignly welcoming could turn out to be fatally alluring, and what seemed fatally alluring could be as kind and friendly as a mother's heart.

The problem, now as always, was to recognize the difference.

It was only with such foresight, and often sheer

luck, that a safe passage through the treacherous country could be negotiated. On his own Ryan was confident that he could make it. However, added to the treachery of nature, he had in tow one of the most black-hearted killers who had ever ridden the Western trails.

Three days ago (but it seemed a hell of a lot longer) he had run Frank Cuskin to ground in a Mexican whorehouse. Cuskin being a gun-slick *hombre*, it was Abe Ryan's good fortune that the killer, due to his preoccupation at the time, was not wearing the double pearl-handled rig with which he had murdered at least twenty men, not including a citizen of Bewley where Abe Ryan toted the marshal's badge, for whose slaying he had come looking for Cuskin. The outlaw was now thirty-six years of age, and he had killed his first man when he was fifteen years old.

'Ain't no way you're goin' to make it, Ryan,' the outlaw predicted confidently. 'Takes a special kinda man to endure the desert, and I figger you ain't got that kinda grit.'

'There's a hangman's noose waiting for your neck back in Bewley, Cuskin,' Ryan said doggedly. 'And I aim to see that you swing from it.'

Cuskin sneered.

'Them's sure brave words, Marshal. But you'll understand if I don't wish my neck to make the

8

acquaintance of that rope you're so keen to see me swing from.'

Abe Ryan held Frank Cuskin's evil, dead eyes.

'The devil is waiting for your soul, Cuskin,' he said with a quite, steely resolve. 'And I aim to deliver it to him. If not at the end of that rope, then at any time along the way.'

For a moment the outlaw's mask of bravado slipped, to reveal the rotten coward that Frank Cuskin really was. The glimpse of fearful doubt he had seen in Cuskin's eyes renewed Abe Ryan's hope of achieving what he'd just promised he would. To press home the upper hand that he had gained, he gave a graphic illustration of a man gagging his last breath at the end of a hanging rope. Ryan's feeling on seeing the blood drain from Cuskin's face (leaving behind the kind of dirty grey seen in river mud at the turning of the tide) was immeasurably pleasurable.

Cuskin's rally was half-hearted.

'You ain't slept in two nights, Ryan. And you've been in the saddle three scorchin' days. How long d'ya figger before you fold, and the buzzards will rip open your belly for all them tasty morsels them critters like so darn much? Pretty soon, I reckon.'

Ryan held the outlaw's evil stare, and delivered a chilling promise:

'Be sure of one thing, Cuskin. I'm going to see you swing at the end of that rope waiting for you back in Bewley.'

'You've got the desert, prowling Indians, and my kin who can't be too far behind to overcome. You ain't got a chance. Quit while you're ahead. Save your hide, man. Ride away.'

'No can do,' Ryan flung back. 'I like to be able to look at myself in the mirror in the morning. If I turned tail, I wouldn't like what I saw a whole lot.'

'You're loco,' Cuskin spat.

'Ain't the first time a fella told me that. Don't waste your breath,' the marshal grated when Cuskin went to speak again. 'My ears are shut. Better get used to the idea. You're on your way to Hades, Cuskin.'

Frank Cuskin wasted his breath anyway.

'The old coot I killed in Bewley was teetering on the edge of eternity anyway. Prob'ly did the old bastard a kindness by finishin' him off. No one will notice he's not around no more. And they'll care less. You're throwin' away your life for nothin', Marshal.'

Abe Ryan's anger was hotter than the sweltering desert.

'That old bastard had been one of the finest, straight-arrow lawmen who ever came down the line, Cuskin. And if Dan Cleary had been a handful of years younger he'd have laid lead in you before you could blink.

'Now, my advice to you is to button your lip, because you're making me real tetchy. And when I get tetchy, my trigger finger begins to itch. And the last thing you need is for me to get an itchy trigger finger, Cuskin. Because if there's the slightest chance that I'm going to topple from my saddle, I'll make full sure that your pump will stop before mine.'

Marshal Abe Ryan edged his horse nearer to Cuskin's.

'Got it?'

The outlaw grinned evilly.

'Somethin' you should know. . . .'

'And what might that be?'

'Sam is part 'Pache.' The Sam he spoke of was Cuskin's oldest brother, one of three, each brother meaner than the other. 'My ma went lookin' for kindlin' to start a fire one day and was waylaid by a buck. My ma always said that it was a terrible thing that happened her. But when she left my pa five years later to hitch her wagon to a no-good ladies' man called Saul Adams, Pa reckoned that her way-laying by that Apache buck was more enjoyable that she ever admitted.'

Cuskin went on: 'Now Sam, bein' the strange sorta *hombre* he is, became real proud of bein' part

11

Indian, especially part 'Pache. So one day he rode right into an Apache village and told them the story of how he came to be. Those murderous critters could see in Sam's face and ways that what he said was true. Now he took a real big chance. They might have decided to split his skull open there and then. But no, they took him in like one of their own. Lived with the 'Pache for a whole two years. Became real friendly. They told him that any time he wanted their help, all he had to do was ask for it.'

As cocky as the only rooster in a henhouse, Cuskin continued: 'Ya know, Marshal. I figger that Sam's already done his askin'. Now knowin' how things are, mebbe you'd want to think again 'bout how dangerous it is for your hide havin' me along. And how you can save it by cuttin' me loose.'

Though concerned by Cuskin's story and the danger posed during the long ride to Bewley, Abe Ryan showed not the merest sliver of that concern when he said, 'That noose is still dangling in Bewley for you, Cuskin.'

'Your funeral, Ryan,' the outlaw drawled, in the manner of a man who did not have a care in the world. But there was no hiding the glint of apprehension in the outlaw's muddy grey eyes.

Had he looked back as he rode ahead, the outlaw would have seen in Abe Ryan's eyes, what

12

the marshal had seen in Cuskin's.

It surely would be one hell of a long ride to Bewley.

CHAPTER TWO

Making their way off the ridge, the shale trail made for precarious progress. A time or two Ryan might have lost his saddle. Had that happened, he had no doubt that Frank Cuskin would have taken full advantage. On the other hand, the marshal could not help having a sneaking admiration for the outlaw's mastery of his horse, learned over twenty years of being continuously in the saddle, chased by one posse or another over desert and plain. Added to all that experience, Cuskin had the seat of a natural horseman that Abe Ryan envied. He was no mean horseman himself but, compared to Frank Cuskin, his skills were lagging far behind.

In the twelve years he had worn the marshal's badge in Bewley, Ryan had not had much call for the kind of long, arduous and tricky ride he was now engaged in. His time in the saddle had been spent visiting the ranches and farms round Bewley, sorting out the feuds and disputes which were inevitable between farmers and cowmen. It had been easy, unchallenging riding, which had ill-prepared him for the journey he had embarked on when he had set out to bring Frank Cuskin to justice; a reckoning he had escaped for far too long while other lawmen, lacking in grit, had turned a blind eye to him and his brothers' misdeeds, or had taken the fistful of dollars which the Cuskin gang had often handed over to sweeten a badge-toter's humour.

Some would say (and there were those in Bewley who had said) that he had been dumb to have sought out Frank Cuskin without the backing of a posse. But he had figured that posses stirred a lot of dust and were easily seen. And if Cuskin missed the posse, there would be no shortage of hardcases who would pass the word along. Outlaws and hardcases acted in concert against the common enemy of the law.

'You might as well shoot yourself right here and now, Abe,' Kate Collins had told him, when he had told her of his plan to track Frank Cuskin on his ownsome. 'You've had some crazy ideas in your time. But trying to get Cuskin's neck in a noose all by yourself is the craziest yet! And so says your good friend Henry Bowdrie.'

Having come to mind, the image of the flame-haired Irishwoman was a mighty difficult one to shift, and the truth of it was that he was in no hurry to shift it. Had he had the courage, he would have got on his knees a long time ago and asked her to marry him. And some day he might at that, before he was too old to do anything useful on the honeymoon. Time was marching steadily on for Kate as well, and it puzzled him why she had not been swept off her feet years ago; there were certainly enough men in Bewley, some with deep pockets too, who would not hesitate to wed and bed her. But, a woman of great independence, Kate had spurned all comers.

He had often been joshed about how he could make Kate smile like no other man could. He thought a lot about why that might be, but never found an answer.

Many times he had stormed out of the marshal's office resolved to pop the question. But by the time he reached her dressmaker's shop, his courage whittled away, he had come up with some lame duck excuse for his visit. His tail between his legs, he'd return to the marshal's office ready to chew iron. When he'd cooled down, he'd promise himself yet again that one day he'd speak his mind and clear the air between him and Kate Collins.

Now, riding tail on Frank Cuskin, through a

narrow canyon, with a passel of dangers ahead, Marshal Abe Ryan wondered if he'd ever get the chance to ask Kate Collins to marry him. And maybe it was best that he never had got up the nerve. Because had he done so, and had she accepted him, she might now be a widow woman very soon.

Frank Cuskin glanced over his shoulder, a sneer making his face more ugly than that of a hungry coyote whose meal had been snatched away.

'Don't ya wonder 'bout who might be lurkin' atop those walls, Marshal?' he said, looking to the top of the canyon. 'An Apache arrow is real silent. Gets ya 'fore you even know you've been got.'

It was something Ryan knew. And it was a reminder that he could have done without; a reminder that sent a trickle of sweat as cold as a dead man's finger along his spine.

'You've still gotta chance to cut me loose.'

Abe Ryan's features set in stone. 'I've got a real keen hankering to see your rotten neck stretched, Cuskin. So I reckon it's worth taking my chances.'

'You're a dumb critter, Ryan,' the outlaw spat spitefully. 'The dumbest bastard I ever knowed.'

Grim-faced, Cuskin rode on, fretting even more than he had when he had last tempted the marshal to take his offer to quit. It worried him that the more he tempted Ryan, the more resolved the lawman became to deliver him to a hangman's rope in Bewley. He knew from long experience that an honest badge-toter was as formidable an adversary as a man could tangle with. And stubbornness added to honesty, made that adversary all the more troublesome to deal with.

Abandoning the idea to persuade Ryan, Cuskin knew there was only one hope left to him, and that was to outwit him. There would be a chance or two along the way – there always was.

All he had to do was be patient, and take that chance when it came.

He had given the marshal a lot of guff about the threat from his brothers and Indians, but that might be all it was – guff – hot air. He and his brothers had had a bust-up after he'd sold a woman they'd been sharing – a woman Sam had gotten a strong yearning for: a long way beyond simple pleasure. So he had figured that putting her out of Sam's reach would also put her out of Sam's mind. Another town, another woman, that would be that. Sam would stop pining, and the trio would get back to their murderous ways.

But the opposite had been the outcome. Now he worried that on hearing of his capture Sam would let him dangle at the end of a rope as retribution for what he'd seen as his youngest brother's treachery. Hank, the second Cuskin brother, might try to assuage Sam's anger, but he did not hold out much hope of that. Hank Cuskin was a mean bastard, but lily-livered when it came to standing up to Sam.

He'd likely go along with what Sam decided.

Down the years, the brothers had ridden together, drunk together, killed, robbed and pillaged together – womanized together, too, until Sam had been smitten. Then his black heart jiggered to a different tune: the tune of love. He'd never have thought it possible until he'd seen Sam act all mushy when he was with the woman. And when he'd made her out of bounds to him and Hank, Sam Cuskin's enchantment had been confirmed. Frank Cuskin had been surprised further when he had spoken to Hank about Sam's changing ways, when Hank had said that he figured they should let Sam be and ride on as a duo. One brother becoming soft-hearted was bad, but both of them was too much. So he'd chosen his own company and ridden on alone. That was how Ryan had snared him in Mexico. Another time the Bewley marshal would have had three Cuskins to deal with. It was a lucky break for Ryan that he'd had only the one.

And, if lucky once, he might get lucky again. That luck might last all the way to Bewley, and that dangling noose.

With so much uncertainty about any possible rescue, all that Frank Cuskin could depend on were his own wits and wiles to help him slip Ryan's clutches. He took comfort from how well those wits and wiles had served him in the past. He'd escaped from a hundred tight corners. He had to believe that he could do it again.

Had Cuskin looked behind him right at that moment, he'd have seen the opportunity he was wishing for.

To Abe Ryan the canyon was spinning wildly and threatening to close in on him. At the back of his befuddled mind, he knew that he was experiencing the ravages of exhaustion, heat, dehydration, and the constant stress of watching Frank Cuskin's every move.

Up ahead, Cuskin swam in and out of the shimmering heat. Sometimes ten feet tall, other times midget-like. Swaying. Bending. Twisting. Racing close, then zooming away in to the distance. Shadows. Near darkness. Then blinding light that bore through into the dark recesses of his brain. Reason told Ryan that what his eyes were telling his brain could not be happening. But that took nothing away from his anxiety and fear.

He grabbed his saddle horn to anchor himself. Were he to topple from his saddle, Cuskin would be on him like a wild beast. He forced himself to breathe deeply, though the hot desert air had few reviving qualities. Slowly, the spinning ceased, and the walls of the canyon stopped their relentless march towards him from either side.

A breeze blew across his face, as if the doors of heaven had opened to favour him. His wooziness eased. His eyes became focused, his grip on the saddle horn more certain. And his legs felt firm again against his horse. His confusion passed. A new freshness spread through him. He had come perilously close to being at Frank Cuskin's mercy, which would be no mercy at all. He had had good fortune. But Abe Ryan knew that there would be other times before he reached Bewley (if he reached Bewley) when he'd be tested by country and man.

Luckily, preoccupied, Frank Cuskin had not looked back: his loss, Ryan's gain.

Thirst, as hot as hell's coals, burned at the back of Ryan's throat, making him conscious of the more empty than full canteen hanging on his saddle horn. His plan had been to fill up at a water hole the day before, only to find it fouled by a rotting coyote when he had reached it, making it necessary to veer off his planned route back to Bewley, to seek water at a mission that acted as a refuge and resting-place for trail-weary travellers. The fouling of the water hole might have been accidental. However, it might also have been malicious.

A lowdown trick by Cuskin's kin to thwart him? Or an accident of nature? Only time would tell.

Since they'd found the water hole unusable Cuskin's confidence had risen, in direct ratio to Ryan's growing unease. Thirst. Exhaustion. Arrow. Bullet. All would have the same result: his bones bleaching in the furnace that was the desert.

'Hot, ain't it, Marshal?' Cuskin said. 'And it's goin' to get hotter. So darn hot that a man's insides begin to swell up, and his eyes begin to pop with the pressure inside his skull.'

'I've crossed the desert before, Cuskin,' Ryan said. 'And come out the other side.'

'Ain't the same as livin' in it, is it? That toughens a man's skin, to keep out some of that awful heat that a townie like you soaks in.'

Abe Ryan knew that what Cuskin said was true. Being a town marshal softened a man, made him cosy. Whereas Cuskin and his brothers had been hiding out in one inhospitable place or another all those years when he'd been ambling around Bewley.

'A man learns to control his thirst too,' Cuskin said.

'I ain't a thirsty fella,' Ryan flung back.

Frank Cuskin drew rein, turned in the saddle

and held Ryan's gaze.

'That a fact?' he scoffed. The marshal wanted to look away, because he knew that in his face Cuskin could see clearly the inner toll that the thirst he had spoken of was taking. 'First time I seen a dead man ridin' a horse, Marshal.'

'Easy, Cuskin!' Ryan warned, when the outlaw turned the mare to face him.

'I don't have to take any chances,' Cuskin said surilly. 'All I gotta do is wait 'til you fall outta your saddle, lawman.'

'You're going to have a hell of a long wait.'

Ryan wished that that were true, but he knew that it wasn't. The reality was that any second, weakened as he was, he could crash to the ground.

'You're welcome to my canteen if you want it.' Cuskin taunted the lawman by telling him. 'Near full. Go down smooth to ease those rusty innards of yours. And all you gotta do is—'

'Not a chance!' Ryan snarled, anticipating the outlaw's price in return for water.

Life held many temptations for a man to stumble over, but right then the biggest temptation that had come down the line for Marshal Abe Ryan was the promise of the water in Frank Cuskin's canteen. Getting his hands on it would mean that he'd make it back to Bewley to pop the question to Kate Collins, the question he'd been wanting to ask since the day she had stepped off the stage four years previously; a question he now regretted not having asked on the numerous times when he'd lost courage and turned tail. The devil was inside his head, telling him that it was as Cuskin had said. Avenging an old man's life was not worth risking the happy years he could spend with Kate. That it would have only been a short time anyway before Dan Cleary would have heard Gabriel's trumpet blow. Ryan had to work hard to resist the Devil's whispering.

'I've got water,' he heard himself say, his words echoing back muzzily from some distant point.

'Sure you have,' Cuskin sniggered. 'But not near enough, Marshal. Not near enough.' He repeated the words cruelly.

'I'll get by.'

'Funny how a man can fool himself, ain't it?' Cuskin said.

'You'll damn well hang, Cuskin,' Abe Ryan said. 'Of that you can be sure.' Ryan slid the Winchester from its saddle scabbard. 'Now move!'

Considering that Ryan might just decide to bring justice forward, Frank Cuskin did as the Bewley marshal ordered. A short way further on shale clattered down. Ryan scanned the top of the canyon to find the source of the disturbance, but could not pin it down. It could have been a natural dislodgement: nothing unusual in that. However, the shale might also have been scattered by human presence. It did not mean a thing that he could not see anyone. Apaches and *hombres* like the Cuskins had a way of remaining invisible until they wanted to be seen. But then if the shale had been dislodged by friends or kin of Frank Cuskin, all it would take was one rifle shot or an arrow to set Cuskin free. It was a consolation that gave only brief respite to the marshal. Because to fatally wound him from on high from a sharp shooting angle, would have taken an ace marksman. The kill would have to be perfect and instant.

Because with a rifle pointing, any misjudgement and Cuskin could catch Ryan's lead.

Cuskin looked to the top of the canyon.

'Kinda scary, ain't it, Marshal?' he crooned. 'Right now you could be in someone's sights.' The outlaw's grin was wide and cocky.

'In that case I reckon it best to kill you right now, Cuskin.'

Marshal Abe Ryan's levelled 'Chester wiped the grin from Cuskin's face and replaced it with the look of a trapped animal.

Frank Cuskin's raw fear gave Abe Ryan immense pleasure. He looked to the top of the canyon and shouted, 'He's a dead man if you so much as break wind!'

Abe Ryan wanted to believe that the sense of eyes watching was just his nerves acting up. But he couldn't quite ignore the ripple of muscle that sent a shiver through him.

'Lots of time yet, Ryan,' Cuskin crowed.

CHAPTER THREE

Smoke!

Abe Ryan drew rein, and ordered his prisoner: 'Take cover in that gully.' It was well into the morning, close to midday. Progress had been slow but steady, every inch of country needing to be reconnoitred for signs of trouble, and trouble was never far away in terrain that was favoured by no end of no-goods criss-crossing the border coming and going to Mexico, and Indians. And even if you were exercising the utmost caution, surprise might never be far away because hostiles, particularly Apaches, could blend in with their surroundings and remain hidden until it was too late. Men like the Cuskins, too, though not as skilful as Indians, quickly learned to remain out of sight, watching the watcher, because every rider could be a lawman seeking them out. Behind any boulder, in any canyon, death by man or beast could be lying in wait, and all the traveller could hope for, if his luck ran out, was that his demise would be swift and merciful.

'Looks like trouble, Marshal,' Cuskin said smugly. 'Smoke in this country usually is.'

'You just keep one thing in mind, Cuskin,' Abe Ryan growled, irked by the outlaw's smugness. 'Death is right on your doorstep. And I won't hesitate to deliver swift justice if it looks like you're going to avoid that rope waiting back in Bewley.'

Cuskin's grin vanished.

'Like I said, you're a dead man riding, Ryan. Ain't no way my neck is goin' to be stretched. This country's got a whole passel of cronies. You've been one hell of a lucky man up to now, but that luck sure won't hold all the way to Bewley. On that you can count, lawman.'

'Shut your mouth, Cuskin!'

Ryan cursed his show of irritation, because it gave an insight into the state of his nerves. Frank Cuskin did not need to say anything. His scoffing grin was back, and that said all that needed to be said.

The Bewley lawman poked his head over the rim of the gully, to look with dour worry at the thick black smoke rising into the clear, copper-coloured desert sky. It was a useless exercise, because it was impossible to judge how distant the smoke was, and between it and him the terrain rose and fell, twisted and turned, keeping its secrets from view. There had been no word of Indian trouble reaching Bewley, but that in fact meant little. Relations between the whites and redman were never far from breaking-point. There were those on both sides who were ever ready to stir trouble, figuring that neither breeds nor creeds could exist side by side, even in the vast country they were part of. For some whitemen and some Indians, too, the only peace possible would come when one of them was no longer around.

'Are we goin' to sit here 'til we roast,' the outlaw enquired inconsequentially of Ryan.

'We'll wait for as long as it takes,' Ryan stated bluntly.

However, he knew that hanging around in the furnace heat of the gully would, in no time at all, take a heavy toll on spirits and strength, more so on his than Cuskin's, he reckoned. The outlaw had an advantage of at least ten years on him in age, and a difference in the poundage he carried, too. It wasn't considerable, but every ounce of flesh needed more water, and every pound of flesh used up more energy to bear it. He could grab Cuskin's water canteen, but the decent streak in Abe Ryan wouldn't allow him to survive on another man's

29

demise. Expecting to be able to refill at the fouled water hole, he had unwisely drunk liberally of his water. So his foolishness made his thirst his problem, and his alone.

Not a word passed between Ryan and Cuskin for a longish spell. Then the outlaw observed: 'That smoke is thinning out. I reckon that whatever ruckus was goin' on has been decided one way or the other.'

'Mebbe,' Ryan mumbled. 'But there's no point in being too hasty.'

'Toss of a coin, ain't it? Ride on, or sit and wait.'

Frank Cuskin had a point. By riding on they could come face to face with whomever Ryan was trying to steer clear of. While staying put, trouble could arrive on his doorstep. It was a dilemma he wished he didn't have to face. But it was there and it was time to decide on what to do. And then pray that he had made the right decision. Making up his mind, Ryan said, 'Time to make tracks.'

Now that the lawman had made his decision, Cuskin niggled away at his determination. 'Sure hope you've called it right, Marshal.' His laughter was mocking. 'I'd sure like to have better company in hell than a badge-toter.'

'Well, I'd hope that I'd be going the other way to where you're headed,' the marshal flung back. 'I'll surely be disappointed if I ain't. Come up easy out of the gully, Cuskin. Blink an eyelid in a fashion I don't like, and you'll be heading to wherever you're going spit quick.'

The outlaw mounted up and scrutinized the marshal closely.

'I ain't that pretty,' Ryan joked.

Frank Cuskin did not share in the joke.

'Ya know, you ain't lookin' too good, Marshal. I figger that all I gotta do is wait.' He pointed to the sky. 'In no time at all I'll be freer than that buzzard.'

Sombrely, Abe Ryan thought that Frank Cuskin might very well be right.

Knowing well Ryan's inner struggle, Cuskin dangled temptation again. 'Any time, Marshal.' He rode on ahead. 'Any time at all.'

They had spent close on an hour in the gully, and the heat had drained most of what little strength Ryan had left. But Frank Cuskin, riding easy and untroubled, had not been and was not now bothered by the gruelling desert heat. He turned in his saddle from time to time to enjoy Ryan's discomfort. The dust, too, was a problem. It clung to Ryan's skin and burned on it, and in some parts through it, causing as much pain as toothache. Under his tongue an abscess was forming, and his throat and lungs burned with the red dust clogging his air passages. Not able to withstand his thirst for a second longer, the lawman ordered Cuskin to hold up while he sipped sparingly from his canteen, making every precious drop count.

Temptingly, Frank Cuskin shook his canteen. The swish of the water in it had Ryan swallowing hard.

'Like I told you, your price is too high, Cuskin,' Ryan said.

'I ain't puttin' a price on it.'

Abe Ryan figured that along with every other bone and muscle in his body, the heat must also be affecting his hearing.

'Come and get it.' Cuskin proffered the canteen. To take it Ryan would have to get closer to Cuskin than was wise.

'I ain't that dumb, Cuskin,' he croaked.

'I'd sling it, but I reckon you ain't in no condition to grab it. It might bust, and all that water soakin' into the earth would be a sure waste.' Cuskin unscrewed the cap of the canteen and drank, letting the water dribble down his chin. Ryan's tortured eyes latched on to every silver trickle of the liquid. 'It sure is sweet, Marshal.'

To load torture on torture, the outlaw spat out a full mouthful of water on to the dry ground, through which it disappeared instantly.

'Yes, sir. Real sweet.'

'You're taking one hell of a risk, Cuskin,' Ryan said, in an intended snarl that came out as a squeak. 'What you've got there is more precious in the desert than pockets full of gold. I might just cut you down for that water canteen.'

'You might,' the outlaw said, 'if you was me. But you ain't got the lack of conscience to allow you to do that.' He took another swig from the canteen. 'Picks ya right up, Marshal.' Again, having washed the water around inside his mouth, Cuskin spat it out.

Abe Ryan's eyes followed the globule of liquid all the way, and, as previously, his burning innards cramped all the more on once again seeing it seep into the moisture-starved dust. The outlaw screwed the canteen cap back on. 'Catch!'

Ryan watched, agonized, as the canteen looped towards him, seeming to be impossibly out of reach, even if he could muster the spit to stand in his stirrups to catch it. At the last second it dropped closer to him and he reached for it, only to find it brush against his grasping fingers tantalizingly close. It sailed past, clattering down among boulders behind him. Despite every ounce of sense in him telling him not to dismount and go in search of the canteen, Ryan did just that.

On his feet, weakened as he was, Cuskin took the opportunity he had engineered. He swung and came at Ryan, his intention to run him down etched in every line of his cruel, cunning face. The marshal tried to sidestep his charge, and might have done so had the heel of his boot not snagged between a pair of rocks embedded in the hard soil. But as it turned out, luck favoured him. His topple sideways took him away from the charging horse, which brushed against him instead of meeting him head on. Luck came to his aid a second time, when the angle at which Cuskin approached took him into a narrow dip. The horse bucked and threw him clear. Cuskin crashed heavily on to a stony patch, and his wind left him in a whoosh. Abe Ryan had the good sense to free his foot from his trapped boot.

Fit as the proverbial fiddle, Cuskin quickly regained his wind, but not quickly enough. It could not have been more than ten seconds in all, but it was sufficient time for Ryan to be on his feet, and as ready as he could be for the outlaw when he regained his, by which time Ryan was putting everything he had into a wide swing that caught Cuskin on the right side of his head. The piledriver spun Frank Cuskin like a top and he reeled away. Ryan knew that were he to allow the better-toned killer time to gather his wits, the chance of him coming out of the fight the winner was not good. On legs that wobbled every which way, and might at any second buckle, all the Bewley lawman had going for him was sheer luck. He knew, as he charged Cuskin, that if the outlaw side-stepped by a couple of inches he'd go right past into the boulders.

And if that happened he was done for.

Cuskin was up and grinning. There was still a sizeable gap to close. Ryan could feel the last vestiges of energy seeping from his legs. It looked like he would not even make it to the outlaw, and all Cuskin needed to do was stand and wait until he folded. However, the evil in Cuskin made him want to hammer Ryan into the ground, so he went to meet him, fists balled, his well-toned muscles tensed, his face grim with a killer's determination

As it turned out, the outlaw's haste to pulverize Abe Ryan was his downfall. For once, the Bewley lawman was glad of his extra poundage as it carried him stumbling in to Cuskin. It was more a helpless fall than a planned lunge, but the result was the same. Cuskin tumbled backwards, legs and arms flailing. Ryan crashed down on top of him, his balled fist connecting with the outlaw's forehead, rattling his brain. Cuskin tried to off-load the marshal, but struggled to do so. Abe Ryan's shovel-like hand grabbed Cuskin by the throat,

Almost instantly, the outlaw's tongue popped out and began to swell, turning purple as it did so.

Ryan elbowed him under the chin and felt a squirt of blood on his face as Cuskin's teeth bit into his tongue. His howl gave Ryan the final push to finish the tussle. While maintaining his grip on Frank Cuskin's throat, Ryan landed a punch that had Cuskin's eyes rolling. And just for safety, the lawman hammered the outlaw's head on a rock. Cuskin lay still, groaning.

Abe Ryan stood up, leaned down and hauled the swaying outlaw to his feet. Then, for good measure, he lined him up and delivered an upper-cut from the ground. 'That, mister,' Ryan said breathlessly, 'should keep you nice and quiet while I go find that canteen.'

While searching among the boulders for the canteen, Abe Ryan had a sense of eyes on him, but he resisted the urge to check his surroundings, choosing to continue his search, hoping that his pretence of unawareness would make the watcher careless, and that he'd pick up the sound of a threat to his well-being, if there was such, before it was too late to act.

Fortunately, finding the canteen did not take long. He picked it up and dusted it off as if he hadn't a care in the world, while letting his gaze drift slowly around, recognizing how futile his survey of his surroundings was. There were a hundred hidey-holes, any one of which could be home to whoever was watching, if in fact anyone was. After days of thirst, heat and sleep deprivation, a man's perception went awry. Imagination took over from reason, trepidation from calm, logic gave way to fuzzy thinking; hearing and sight began to play tricks. Instincts became blurred, and left the way open for uncertainty to creep in.

There was nothing practical that he could do. If there was a threat, all he could do was hope that when it finally materialized he'd have time to deal with it.

Frank Cuskin was coming too, sitting up groggily, holding his head. Abe Ryan went to him, on legs that were still trying to recover from slugging it out with the outlaw.

'You near busted my skull,' Cuskin raged.

'You got what you deserved, Cuskin,' Abe Ryan flung back harshly, having no sympathy for the killer. 'In fact I wouldn't have minded one little jot if I had. And maybe I should have. But I've got this image in my mind of you swinging from that rope waiting for you in Bewley.'

'You're loco, Ryan,' Cuskin spat. 'Right now my eyesight is scattered somethin' awful. But I can still see that you're about all in, lawman.'

'I'll admit that I ain't in the best shape I've ever been in, Cuskin. But I'll make it to Bewley with you in tow. Count on it. Now get back in the saddle!'

'I ain't in no shape to get back in no saddle,' the outlaw groused.

'OK,' Ryan said with false friendliness.

'That's better,' Cuskin snorted, reading the marshal's false friendliness as capitulation, a delusion which Abe Ryan quickly shattered.

'The way I see it is, you've got two choices, Cuskin. You ride. Or. . . .' Frank Cuskin's prominent Adam's apple bobbed like a cork on choppy water when Abe Ryan drew and pointed his six-gun. 'Here and now I save Bewley the cost of stringing you up.'

'You're a lawman,' Cuskin fretted. 'That badge says that you don't shoot a man in cold blood.'

'True,' the marshal said. 'But, you see, you ain't a man, Cuskin. You're a wild, murdering, no-good bastard. In my book you're no better than vermin. And there's only one way to deal with vermin.'

Abe Ryan cocked the six-gun, his features set in stone.

'What's it to be, Cuskin?'

With a scowl that would put legs under Satan, Frank Cuskin mounted up, promising: 'I'm goin' to enjoy skinnin' you alive, Ryan.'

'I don't plan on giving you that chance, Cuskin,' the marshal flung back. 'Now make tracks nice and easy. No jerky movements.'

A short distance on Abe Ryan realized that the

eyes that he had sensed watching him were probably those of the blood-soaked man who stumbled into their path.

Startled, Ryan drew rein. 'Hold up,' he commanded Cuskin. 'And don't get up to any trickery, or I'll cut you down for sure and be done with it.'

Though his sympathy went out to the stricken man, Ryan's approach was still cautious. He had learned from long experience not to trust appearances. The man seemed to be in bad shape, but the trickery of men like Cuskin and his kind knew no limits of inventiveness.

'Help me,' the man croaked, bloodstained hands reaching out. 'Please, mister,' he pleaded with Ryan. The blood gurgling in his thoat excaped his lips and ran down his chin, dropping in great scarlet gobblets on to the dry dusty earth at his feet.

Abe Ryan, compassionate man that he was, could no longer resist giving the man the help he pleaded for. He leaped from the saddle just in time to catch the man as he folded, past helping. Eyes, clouded by oncoming death, locked with the marshal's. The man's mouth formed words that were never to be spoken. The dullness in his eyes intensified, seeping through them like black glutinous mud until they became lifeless orbs, staring vacantly into eternity – peaceful eyes, the hurt and pain in them gone. Ryan laid him gently on the arid ground; the congealing blood was already attracting masses of flies to his wounds. The ravenous swarm filled the dead man's mouth, making it seem that something dark and evil was rising up from within him.

The stench of death was already taking hold.

Though the man was older than when he had last seen him, Ryan recognized Doc Murray, the proprietor of a travelling medicine wagon which had visited Bewley some years before.

'Leave him be,' Cuskin said, and, in response to Abe Ryan's look of contempt, added: 'He's dead. Nothin' you can do.'

'I can give him the best burial I can,' the marshal growled. 'And that's what I aim to do, Cuskin.'

'You're loco. Smoke risin'. Now this. Not the time to hang 'round.'

'Indians, you reckon?'

'Don't reckon. I know.'

'Why should that worry you?' Ryan asked of the outlaw. 'Apaches are friends with you and your kin. So you shouldn't come to any harm.'

Frank Cuskin ran his tongue over suddenly parched lips, and his eyes held the spectre of terror.

'Ain't so,' he confessed. 'It's true that my

40

brother Sam's got 'Pache blood, and for a spell was real cosy with them black-hearted killers. But he messed up real bad. He took one of their women without her say-so. My brother Sam is a lusty *hombre*. When he feels, he feels, and takes. Truth is, I spun you a long-legged yarn, Ryan. I was hopin' that, scared, you'd cut and run.'

Frank Cuskin looked round furtively. It pleased Abe Ryan to see the killer sweat, like so many of the men he'd laid low must have done.

'No matter now,' Cuskin whined. 'We've got to save our scalps.'

'Well, I figure that you've got a whole lot more to worry about than me,' Ryan said. 'You being a Cuskin.'

'What good will it do wastin' time plantin' him?' the outlaw grumbled.

'In my book, a man's got a right to a decent burial,' Abe Ryan said sternly. 'Now get used to the idea that this man is being buried. Makeshift as that burial will be.'

'Then you must let me help.'

'Help?' Ryan's voice reeked of scepticism. 'You ain't the helping kind, Cuskin. I figure that maybe you'd like to get your hands on a rock to open my skull with. Or maybe my gun to blow a hole in me with. Now, while I'm doing what I have to do, you keep your eyes peeled.' Though he was feeling far

41

from humorous, Ryan chuckled. 'We wouldn't want a bunch of angry, bloodthirsty Apaches getting their hands on those pretty locks of yours.'

'Just get on with it!'

There was not much by way of a decent burial that Abe Ryan could manage. All he could do was lay Doc Murray out, mumble a few words of commendation to the Almighty, and cover him with rocks. The rocks would not be much of a protection for Murray's mortal remains. In no time at all the desert's four-legged and winged predators would expose the body and feast on it. But at least he'd know that he'd done what little he could do.

Riding away, Abe Ryan glanced back at the makeshift grave, its only mark a ragbag cross of scrub held together with the doc's bootlace. Not a lot at the end of a man's life. Ryan reckoned that he would not even have as much, if death in the desert was to be his fate.

CHAPTER FOUR

The desert heat was now at its most intense, and both man and beast laboured to withstand its onslaught – even Frank Cuskin was beginning to wane somewhat. Or maybe it was not the heat that was subduing the outlaw's spirit, but the steady, relentless progress against all the odds that was being made to reach Bewley and the fate that awaited him.

On starting out, Cuskin had been in no doubt at all that the task facing the Bewley marshal would be one too great to accomplish, but in another ten miles or so they would arrive at the mission that Ryan had set his sights on. There they would get sustenance from the monks and full water canteens and, hopefully, a couple of hours rest before cutting east to the old outlaw trail by which Ryan hoped to reach Bewley – that was if the trail was still there at all and, if it was, that it would be in a fit condition to travel along.

Trails came and went, falling out of favour when new trails were cut that were shorter or safer. Harkin's Way, the trail he was headed for, had been named in memory of the Reverend Jess Harkin, a preacher who had tried to bring the word of God to the Indians (unwisely at a time in which redman and white settler were in the middle of a full-blown war), and had ended up drawn and quartered.

The mistake the reverend had made was to think that reason would prevail, once red and white man understood each other. But he discovered to his cost that neither side was of a mind to listen, seeing as the only solution was the complete and total annililation of the enemy. Some folk saw Jess Harkin as a saint for his efforts at reconciliation, while others reckoned that he was loco to have thought that savages, as whitemen saw the Apache, and vice versa, could ever have been persuaded to live together.

Time had since marched on, and Indians and settlers had, in the main, come to live together, except for the odd outbreak of hostilities. However it was a brittle truce, brought about by the weariness of war, which was sometimes breached by misunderstanding, and sometimes (Abe Ryan thought of the smoke he'd seen) by troublemakers whose only motive was selfishly to serve their own ends. When that happened, skirmishes would be the order of the day until someone talked sense.

During these times all white men and Apaches became the enemy, each to the other, and the bloodletting became indiscriminate: all a man had to be was white or red, and unlucky enough to be in the wrong place at the wrong time. The desert was a strange place. A man could ride for days, weeks, even months and not meet another soul. On the other hand, round any twist in the trail a man could meet an enemy and sudden death. All a body could hope for (as Abe Ryan was hoping for now) was that his name was not on a bullet or an arrow.

At first, preoccupied as he was, Ryan did not see the woman wandering aimlessly towards them, raw terror etched in every dust-caked line of her face. On hearing the clop of hoofs, she stopped dead in her meandering tracks, her face taking on a new terror. 'Please,' she wailed, 'don't hurt me.'

Abe Ryan leaped from the saddle and went quickly to the woman's assistance. She looked about her wildly and backed away, holding up her hands to ward him off, stumbling blindly. Ryan realized that the woman was blind.

'Easy, ma'am,' he said calmly. 'I mean you no harm.'

'Who are you?' she questioned, seemingly in panic.

'I'm a lawman, ma'am. The marshal of Bewley. The name's Abe Ryan.'

'I've heard of you.'

Ryan grinned. She'd not see it, but he figured that she'd hear it in his voice when he spoke. 'Good, I hope?'

The woman smiled.

'All good, sure enough.' Her head jerked. 'There's another man? I can smell him.'

Ryan laughed. 'Kind of ripe, ain't he? But you're safe.'

Her apprehension flooded back. 'I sense that he's not a good man, Marshal Ryan.'

'Don't worry me what you think,' Frank Cuskin grunted.

Ears cocked, the blind woman tracked his voice.

'I've heard that voice before,' she said fearfully. 'In a saloon, maybe?'

'A saloon, ma'am?' Abe Ryan queried.

'I used to be a saloon singer, Marshal,' the woman explained, in response to the surprise in Ryan's voice.

'I'd never have figured you for a saloon singer, ma'am.'

'When my man was gunned down, I had to make ends meet as best I could. Then soon after, for no

46

reason that anyone can say, my eyes began to fail me. Until my world went dark, Marshal.'

'Tough break, ma'am.'

'God's ways are not ours to understand.'

'Gunned down, you say?'

'Larry worked for Fargo. He was delivering a cash-box to the bank in Pewter's Crossing a couple of years ago. . . .' Abe Ryan recalled the robbery for which no one had been brought to justice. The woman had to be Larry Begley's wife, the Fargo courier. 'I was in Pewter's Crossing, to get material to make new curtains. I was to meet Larry there,' she said reflectively.

'You're Adeline Begley, then?'

'Yes, Marshal. You knew my husband?'

'Yes, ma'am. Nice feller. Shared a bottle a couple of times when storms struck and made it unsafe for the stage to go on. I was real sorry to hear that he'd been shot down.'

Adeline Begley was not listening to the marshal. Her unsighted attention was focused on Frank Cuskin.

'I know where I heard that voice before,' she stated, a shiver in her voice. 'It wasn't in a saloon. It was in Pewter's Crossing. The day Larry was murdered.' She grabbed Abe Ryan by the arm, trembling in fear. 'That's the voice of the man who cut my husband down without mercy, and in cold

47

blood, Marshal Ryan.'

'I asked him real nice to hand over the cash-box, ma'am,' Cuskin snorted. 'Dumb critter wouldn't. So I shot him. Seemed the only thing to do.'

'Who is he, Marshal?' Adeline Begley asked.

'His name is Frank Cuskin, ma'am. He's my prisoner. On his way to a gallows in Bewley.'

'A gallows. That's the best news I've heard in a long, long time, Marshal.' She turned to face Cuskin. 'I hope they hang you high and let you rot dangling, Cuskin. If I had eyes to see with, and a gun to hold, you wouldn't have to risk your hide hauling that bastard all the way to Bewley, Marshal Ryan. But right now I need your help, Marshal.'

'You've got it ma'am. What I can't figure out is what you're doing way out here?'

Then, before she spoke, the penny dropped. She had come from the same direction as Doc Murray had come.

Tears flooded her eyes. 'It was awful. We got attacked, Marshal.'

'Doc Murray and you?'

'The doc was kind enough to take me on. I'd sing and he'd sell. Worked real well, too.'

'Had Doc still got his "Gee-up" medicine,' Ryan enquired humorously.

Adeline Begley laughed.

'Couldn't brew it fast enough. Best seller Doc had.'

'It's pure magic, Marshal,' Murray had once confided to Abe Ryan, when the good doc had had to spend a night in the Bewley jail for his own safety, having paid a personal visit with a bottle of his *gee-up* elixir to a lady whose husband happened to be out of town, but whose plans had brought him back into town when the good Doc, naked as Adam in the Garden, was sharing his elixir with the lady who was a very delectable Eve. Considering how dumbstruck the lady had been after Murray had taken a single swallow of his *Gee-up* elixir, it seemed likely that among his array of cure-alls of doubtful merit, there was one of undoubted potency.

The doc, having, by Abe Ryan's intervention, survived the murderous wrath of the cuckolded husband, bridges had been mended the very next morning when the husband dropped by the jail, frayed at the edges by exhaustion to thank Doc and to purchase a crate of *Gee-up*. Having secured the magic potion, the man reminded Doc Murray, none too gently, that were he to see him in Bewley again, a visit to his wife would not be taken kindly. Doc obviously took his advice, because he had not, as instructed, returned.

And he certainly would not be returning now.

Doc Murray had always had a female looker to persuade the men, whom he thought easier to fool once their blood was up, to buy his potions, most of which plain water could match. But uncharitable as it might be to think so, Abe Ryan could not see how a blind woman could be of use in hooking Doc's male customers. They could, of course, look and admire. But for her part Adeline Begely could not lure with her eyes the way a sighted woman can.

'Did you come across Doc, Marshal?'

'Yes, ma'am, I did.' Adeline Begley's eyes filled up as she heard this. 'There was nothing I could do to help. I planted him as best I could.'

'Will you be kind enough to lead me to where Doc is buried, Marshal? I'd like to say a prayer.'

'Sure, ma'am.'

He gave her his arm, and took her back the short distance to where Murray lay. She murmured quietly there for a short while.

Abe Ryan was faced with a dilemma he'd rather not have had. Having to watch every move Frank Cuskin made was a full-time job, without having responsibilty for Adeline Begley to add to his troubles. However, he could hardly leave a blind woman alone in the desert. It had not been long since Doc Murray had put in an appearance, but even in that time it was a miracle that a blind woman had survived in such a treacherous place.

'Can you tell me what happened, ma'am?' Ryan enquired.

'Men came. . . .'

'White men?'

'Yes. Doc was on his own. I had to answer a call of nature. The men did not see me. And Doc, bless his soul, never said I was around.'

'That was very fortunate for you, ma'am.'

'Yes. It was most fortunate, Marshal. When they left, Doc said that he'd try and get help. Where he thought he might find it, I don't know. I knew he was cut up badly, but I never thought he'd die.'

'I'm headed to the mission, ma'am,' Ryan said. 'You come along.'

'How can I thank you?'

'I can think of some ways,' Cuskin sniggered.

'Shut your dirty mouth, Cuskin,' Ryan snarled. 'Any reason why they should have set upon Murray, that you know of?' Ryan asked. 'Other than sheer bloody-mindedness?'

'We'd been in River Gulch a couple of days ago. Doc sold a lot of medicine. I reckon they came looking for his poke, Marshal.'

'That's a good enough reason, I guess. The thing is, if they tracked Doc from River Gulch, then they'd have known you were with him, ma'am. Which is a bit of a puzzler that they didn't go looking for you.'

Adeline Begley shrugged her elegant shoulders.

'It's surely a mystery, Marshal.'

Abe Ryan said, 'Being a lawman, mysteries don't settle very well with me. Makes me kind of edgy, ma'am.'

'Maybe there's no mystery at all. . . .'

'How would that be, ma'am?'

'Doc Murray was a man of moody ways. We had a bust-up in River Gulch. Bust-ups with Doc were nothing new. We patched it up outside of town, but only Doc and me knew that. The men who followed us would not have known about Doc's and my reunion. So ain't it reasonable to assume that when they found Doc alone, they found what they expected to find?'

'It's an explanation, I guess,' Abe Ryan said.

'Sounds like you think there might be another, Marshal Ryan. I'd sure like to hear what it is.'

'Enough of the gab,' Frank Cuskin grumbled. 'Those coyotes who killed Murray must still be in this neck of the woods.'

'Hate to admit it. But the murdering bastard's got a point, Marshal,' Adeline Begley hissed.

Frank Cuskin's response was venomous.

'Ya know, that man of yours was real dumb the way he kept holdin' on to that Fargo box. But mebbe he knew I'd kill him anyway.'

'If I had eyes to see with, Cuskin, I'd pluck yours from their sockets right now,' Adeline Begley raged.

Cuskin scratched his stubbled chin.

'Ya know, Marshal. I figger the blind woman ain't worth the trouble. I say let her be for coyote or buzzard bait.'

'Mrs Begley comes with us, Cuskin,' said Ryan.

'Well then, let's git,' Cuskin said surlily.

'You're in a mighty hurry all of a sudden to make your acquaintance with that hanging rope in Bewley, Cuskin,' Ryan observed thoughtfully.

'If it gets Cuskin's neck in that noose sooner rather than later, Marshal,' Adeline Begley said, 'then do as he says and let me be.'

'Shut your mouth, blind woman!' Cuskin barked. 'I ain't goin' to swing on no rope. And I gotta a real long memory. I don't aim to forget you. So you can expect me to be droppin' by one day,' he threatened.

Adeline Begley's look was one of raw fear.

'Never you mind, ma'am,' Abe Ryan said. 'As sure as day becomes night, one way or another Frank Cuskin is on his way to hell.'

'That's real comforting to know, Marshal Ryan,' she said. 'And I hope hell's fires will be at their hottest ever when he roasts in them!'

*

A short way along, in a small box canyon, they came upon Doc Murray's wagon. Ryan reined in and waited. The first thing he noticed was the wet ground under the medicine wagon. He could forget the water he had hoped to secure from the wagon's water barrel. Why would the men who killed Murray damage the barrel? Water was a gift in the desert, not to be wasted.

'There's nothing to fret about,' Adeline Begley reassured Ryan. 'The men who did for Doc are long gone with his poke. Doc made quite a penny selling his *Gee-up* medicine. The men of River Gulch were real keen to get their hands on it. Seems,' Adeline Begley chortled, 'that it makes a man real loving. If you get my drift, Marshal?'

'Are we goin' to hang 'round here all day?' Frank Cuskin complained grumpily.

'Maybe we should camp here for the night.' The suggestion was Adeline Begley's.

'Night's a long way off,' Ryan said. 'With a touch of luck we can still make it to the mission before nightfall. Or at least a sizeable chunk of the way.'

'Don't like to douse your hope, Marshal,' Begley said, 'but I heard tell that the mission is no more. That the monks have moved on.'

'Who said?' Ryan asked.

'A Bible-thumper me and Doc crossed paths with a couple of days ago. Figured we might be making our way there, so his good deed was to set us straight.'

The news, if it was true, was a bad turning point in the Bewley lawman's plans. He'd been counting on the mission for refreshement and respite. If the mission was no longer there it made an already hard job near to an impossible one. The next water hole he knew of was a day's ride to the north of where he now was, much of it across open, flat country where there was nowhere to hide; the kind of country that a man on a mission such as his, was the last place he'd want to be. But the water hole at Benton Creek was a good, reliable one. The mission, too, had good water, but if it had been abandoned, the chances were that the untended well would have gone sour. So the choice was between risking disappointment at the mission, or making the long, scorching, energy-sapping trek to Benton Creek. It was a choice he wished he did not have to make.

Abe Ryan was not a gambling man, and his first thought was to opt for the more certain Benton Creek. However, the country to the mission had lots of cover and varied terrain, unlike the flat country to Benton Creek wherein a fly would be hard-pushed to find cover. But at Benton Creek it was surefire that he'd be able to replenish their canteens. Whereas if it was as Adeline Begley said, and the mission was no more, Ryan thought bleakly that completing the ride to Bewley might become too hard a task to complete.

He decided on Benton Creek.

Ryan doubted if he'd find a more secure campsite than the box canyon. A campsite that would give cover to light a fire might not present itself again.

'We'll camp here,' he said. 'Come sunup, we'll start out for Benton Creek.'

'Sense at last,' Cuskin grunted.

Ryan's decision obviously found favour with the outlaw. And that gave the marshal a sneaky cause for concern. Perhaps he had made the wrong choice, he considered? Cuskin's satisfaction with his decision to head for Benton Creek probably stemmed from him thinking about the open country they'd have to cross, every inch of it leaving them exposed and vulnerable, greatly easing the task of any searchers for Cuskin.

Something else niggled.

Why had Adeline Begley only mentioned now that the mission was no more? Why had she not said so earlier when he spoke of it?

Strange that she had not.

His concerns might have the substance of a ghost. But Abe Ryan would prefer not to have them at all. But he had one definite and substantial worry. That was that Begley would have to double up with him, on a nag that had difficulty enough carrying one rider.

As on previous nights, Abe Ryan's rest was uneasy. While escorting a man of Cuskin's cunning, not all eventualities could be foreseen or planned for. All Ryan could hope for was time to counter any threat from Cuskin before it was too late. He should never have set out alone to hunt down Cuskin. The longer the return journey to Bewley took, the more probable it became that Frank Cuskin would escape the hangman's rope. Time had been lost, hardship and danger increased, when the water hole he had counted on had been fouled.

He had had his fair share of hard riding in his time, but since he'd become the law in Bewley, the effects of the softer life of a town marshal were now coming home to roost. Days and nights in Bewley (except for the odd Saturday night rowdiness) were calm and quiet. Now and then a hardcase or two happened by, but with little or no easy pickings to be had they soon lost interest and moved on without too much push and shove.

Cuskin, too, would probably have followed the same route had his horse not side-swiped Dan Cleary. Cuskin was uncaring. Cleary was cantankerous. Their combined bad temper had led to irascible exchanges. Cleary's dressing-down of Cuskin brought the outlaw's meaness to the fore, and he reacted in a manner that was ingrained in him. He shot the old-timer, as he would have shot any other man who riled him.

Ryan had been out of town at the time, sorting out a dispute between a couple of ranchers, each claiming ownership of unbranded strays. On returning to town, and hearing what had happened, he figured that Frank Cuskin had acted murderously. Cleary might have shot his mouth off too much (which no one would deny he did from time to time), but in Abe Ryan's book that did not justify a killing, and that made Cuskin's act one of murder, answerable to the law.

It would have been up to a jury to decide on the merits or demerits of the shooting, but Cuskin, on account of his long history of outlawry, had been in no position to risk facing judge and jury, so he'd cut and run, wounding several other townsfolk in his charge out of Bewley, leaving Abe Ryan with no option but to hunt him down and bring him back to face retribution.

'Sweet dreams, Marshal.' Cuskin chuckled, settling down to sleep. 'You be careful now, you hear?' His chuckle became outright laughter, deeply mocking in nature. 'You'd be surprised how many healthy fellas die in their sleep.'

Abe Ryan let the taunt pass.

The moon rose and rode high in the sky, giving welcome illumination to the campsite beyond the glow of firelight, where the desert's predators might lurk. A time or two Ryan had seen the flash of watching eyes in the brief spells when the moon ducked behind a drifting cloud. At intervals Ryan stoked the fire to keep hungry predators at bay. As the sleepless night wore on, it became increasingly cold; a chill that, when added to the cold of exhaustion, seeped deep into the marshal's marrow. Thoughts of nights spent in a feather bed back in Bewley compounded Abe Ryan's disgruntlement with his lot.

Mutterings from within the medicine wagon, where Adeline Begley was sleeping, got Ryan's attention: mutterings that became more and more strident and fraught. She was obviously having a nightmare, and was it any wonder? Ryan went to reassure the blind woman that she was safe. He lifted the wagon flap, and stars exploded in front of his eyes, before he stumbled backwards, poleaxed. The night swam round him, his head fit to explode with the force of the blow it had received. Through a red haze he saw Adeline Begley leap from the wagon and run to Frank Cuskin who was already on his feet to welcome her into his arms in what was obviously a joyous reunion. How could a blind woman run like that, the marshal wondered? But even with an army of demons dancing inside his skull, he knew the answer as soon as the question arose.

He had been the fool of all fools.

Adeline Begley had been faking blindness!

CHAPTER FIVE

Frank Cuskin was standing over Abe Ryan, his boot arrogantly on the marshal's chest. Weak and confused as he was, Ryan's humiliation, sour as gall as it was, had to be put up with. The woman danced and pranced about, revelling in the praise the outlaw poured upon her.

'Not such a tough *hombre* now, are ya, Marshal,' Cuskin taunted. 'Laid low by a little woman! I'd like you to meet Belle Boothley, the best little actress who ever came down the line. Take a bow, Belle.'

Belle Boothley curtsied, then giggled.

'Gee, Marshal Ryan, you seem to have two heads. And you've got eyes looking diff'rent ways.' She bent down and picked up the rock with which she had pulverized Ryan. 'You know, honey,' she said to Cuskin. 'Maybe I should re-set the marshal's eyes.'

'I've got a better idea,' Cuskin said. He pulled her close and whispered something in her ear, much to the amusement of both.

Boothley dropped the rock.

'I like that idea a whole lot better, honey,' she told Cuskin.

Though in more trouble than he'd ever been, Abe Ryan had to admit that as a pair they had engineered the perfect trap. If he lived to be a hundred, which was unlikely, the fact that he had not cottoned on would gall him every second of every day.

Boothley goaded him.

'I was south of the border, a town a couple miles up the line from where you got the jump on Frank. Word travelled fast. Luckily, Doc Murray was passing through, so I glad-eyed the old coot. By the time we reached River Gulch, Doc was ready to do my bidding.

'I fretted something awful, Frank. Thinking I'd never find you. It was a real needle in a haystack. Then, out of the blue, Doc and me came across an old prospector who talked about two riders he'd seen from atop a canyon. . . .'

Abe Ryan recalled the slide of shale that had alerted him.

'I persuaded Doc to hook up with you fellas, telling him that, if we had to fight off any trouble which might come our way, the more guns we had the better. It made sense to Doc. Going in the direction the prospector said you were headed, when we happened on the box canyon I persuaded Doc to wait up until you fellas came along. I knew about what happened at Pewter's Crossing. I also knew that Begley had visited Bewley. I figured that you'd have crossed paths with Begley, Marshal. So I had this great idea. I'd become Adeline Begley. Only I'd be a helpless Adeline.' She laughed. 'Helpless until my chance came along.'

'Brains and beauty rolled into one,' Cuskin said. 'What more could a fella ask for?'

Belle Boothley went on: 'Plans hatched, I kept lookout for you gents, while Doc napped. When I spotted you headed our way, all that needed doing was to do for Doc. But not so as he couldn't come looking for help from you fellas.'

'You must have had Doc wrapped round your little finger,' Ryan observed. 'Doc Murray could be a crusty customer. Wonder what you did to make him so cooperative?'

Suspicion flashed in Frank Cuskin's eyes; eyes that bore into Belle Boothley.

'Yeah. Doc was real cooperative.'

Boastful of her achievements, Boothley was oblivious of Cuskin's jealous suspicion. 'It was easy.

Doc could never resist the company of an obliging lady.'

Cuskin's face purpled with rage. 'That a fact?'

The penny dropped for Boothley. 'Nothing happened between Doc and me, honey,' Belle assured him quickly, before the outlaw cut loose with one of his clenched fists. 'I kept him sweet with promises, that's all.'

'If I thought—'

'Then don't think. No need.' Belle Boothley cuddled up to Cuskin. 'You're my man, Frank. Ain't another like you, honey.'

'She is a good actress, ain't she, Cuskin?' Ryan said, with a mouth that seemed full of cotton, hoping to cause a rift between the pair that he could exploit.

'Shuddup, Ryan,' Cuskin bellowed. 'That's my woman you're doin' down!'

It was a spirited defence of Belle Boothley, but Ryan was not fooled. There was a deadly tension in Cuskin that could swing either way. Neither was Belle Boothley fooled by his defence of her. She figured that Frank Cuskin was buying time to sort out truth from lies, and she was fearful that when he took time to think unemotionally, he'd reason that a woman like her (who liked the company of a man too much to hang around him for a couple of days without sparks flying), travelling with Doc

Murray who had a reputation as a ladies' man, with several cases of *Gee-up* elixir to hand, two and two would make a perfect four.

'I bet that along the way Doc slugged some of his come-hither medicine, Belle,' Ryan said. 'Could put fire in a dead man's loins, I hear.'

Cuskin swung a boot into Abe Ryan's ribs, but the resulting pain was worth it, if his plan to divide and conquer worked.

'I heard 'bout the Doc's elixir, Belle,' the outlaw barked, his jealousy raw and ugly now. 'And I also know how you like a man to pleasure ya. A cat in heat. That's you!'

The slap across the face that Frank Cuskin gave Belle Boothley had the crack of a rifle shot. She flung herself at him, but not with claws unsheathed, as Ryan had hoped. Instead she clung simperingly to Cuskin, currying favour.

'Can't you see what that bastard is doing, Frank, honey? He's trying to turn us against each other, that's what.'

She tried to kiss him, but he pushed her away so hard that she fell on the stony ground. If proof was ever needed that hell hath no fury like a woman scorned, it was on view right there. Ryan could only wish that Belle Boothley had a six-gun to hand, becaue if she had, Frank Cuskin would have bitten the dust right then and there. But, like most men who wanted to believe a woman, he wavered in his resolve to cast her out.

He hurried to help her up.

'Belle, honey, I don't know what got into me. Ya must forgive me. Won't you forgive me?' he whined. Belle Boothley, knowing that she had regained the upper hand, with female cunning only slowly let go of her anger after several more anguished pleas by Cuskin, and only then when Cuskin was at his most grovelling.

'Of course I forgive you, Frank,' she said, her voice full of soft seduction. 'If me and Doc had cosied up to each other, why would I slash him to within an inch of his life with a Bowie? I did it all for you, honey,' she cooed.

She drew him to her, pressing hard against Cuskin, who melted like snow in a furnace. Her womanly wiles fully exercised, she looked over the outlaw's shoulder to Abe Ryan, her smile one of naked triumph, before it changed to one of malicious intent.

The Bewley marshal knew that the price to pay for his failed attempt at sowing the seeds of division, would be high. It did not take long for Belle Boothley to state that price.

'Honey,' she gently disengaged from Cuskin, whose sole thought was to carnally possess Belle Boothley, 'later.'

Cuskin was not pleased.

Abe Ryan tried to revive the friction between the pair.

'I guess Belle's kinda worn out right now, Cuskin,' he said. 'I heard tell that Doc Murray was a man with ferocious appetites that would wear out a woman a whole lot younger than Belle.'

'Easy, Frank,' she counselled, when anger once again sparked the outlaw. 'The marshal is just trying out an old, tired and useless trick.'

'Yeah. Sure, Belle. Yeah.' He chuckled.

Abe Ryan knew that there were no more cards in the deck to be played. Belle Boothley had brains, beauty, and age-old know-how which she had used with the expertise of a woman who had fooled a lot of men, and would fool many more before her charms waned. Why she had risked all for Cuskin he was at a loss to know. She could have had any man. All she had to do was crook her finger. Perhaps Belle Boothley was the kind of woman who liked to live dangerously and around danger. Danger aplenty would be her lot with Frank Cuskin.

'Now . . .' Belle Boothley strolled to where Abe Ryan was lying, still groggy. 'What do you reckon we should do with the marshal, Frank?'

'Kill him, of course!'

'That's surely a good idea,' Belle said. 'But

there's a whole mess of ways to skin a cat, honey.'

Frank Cuskin's grin was as mean as a rattler's spit.

'I bet you've got somethin' real entertainin' in mind, Belle.'

'Well, something's come to mind that I kind of like, honey,' she said, her smile full of the devil's mischief.

'I bet it has,' the outlaw encouraged. Then, eagerly: 'Don't keep it all to yourself, Belle. I'm sure the marshal would like to hear.'

Belle Boothley laughed throatily. 'Oh, I don't think so, honey.'

Frank Cuskin's eyes lit up. 'That mean, huh?'

'Even meaner, Frank.

The outlaw's spite-filled laughter filled the small box canyon. When he finally stopped laughing, he said, 'Do tell, Belle, darlin'.'

'Well, I think we should hogtie the marshal to a wagon wheel. Leave him be. Come dark, with no fireglow, in no time at all the four-legged hungry desert dwellers will be competing with each other to rip out the his innards.'

'Ain't she a real peach of a woman, lawman?' Cuskin bragged. 'Learned that fancy way of talkin' when she was a schoolmarm.' He swaggered, and pulled Belle Boothley to him roughly, the way he might a saloon woman, bought and paid for. 'That was before I opened the kinda doors a man like me can, to bring out the real woman hidin' behind the schoolmarm. Ain't no goin' back to blackboard and chalk now, is there, honey?'

'Not a chance, Frank,' she said, her eyes adoring.

'You'd do anythin' for me, honey, wouldn't ya?'

The adoration in Belle Boothley's eyes intensified.

'You just ask, Frank,' she panted. 'And I'll surely do.'

Cuskin went to retrieve his gunbelt from Ryan's saddle-bag and buckled it on. 'Sure feels good,' he said. 'Felt kinda naked without it.' He turned to Belle Boothley, took her in his arms and kissed her long and hard, leaving her breathless with the rivers of passion coursing through her. 'Just ask, huh?' He slid the six-gun from its holster, and held it out for Belle to come and take. 'Shoot the marshal. Right 'tween the eyes.'

Mesmerized by the outlaw's raw sexualilty, and the equally potent force of her own desires, Belle Boothley proved to be as good as her word. She took the six-gun, and came to stand in front of Abe Ryan.

She levelled the gun and cocked the hammer.

'You say when, Frank,' she said, totally Cuskin's to control and manipulate.

In the seconds before his death, Marshal Abe Ryan knew the veracity of a man's life flashing before him, from boyhood to manhood, good times, bad times, and indifferent times through which he had drifted aimlessly, like a ship without a rudder. Sometimes he'd seemed to have no purpose in life other than getting through another aimless dreary day as fast as was possible, seeking to lighten the darkness of the time with anything to hand which would, however temporarily and fleetingly, lift his spirits or ease his pain. There had been many such wasted days, which he now regretted, too late. So, in his final seconds, he turned his mind to the good times he had had, gave thanks for them, and wished he had treasured the good times and ditched the bad.

In the main, he hoped that folk would remember him for the good he'd done.

CHAPTER SIX

Frank Cuskin gloated, every inch of him mocking Ryan with the contempt of victor for vanquished. 'Well now, lawman, ain't the tables really been turned?' He came and stood over Ryan. 'All that gab 'bout stringin' me up, and here you are,' he kicked the lawman squarely in the ribs, 'as helpless as a kitten up a tree.'

He sniggered maliciously.

'Ya know, Belle. Mebbe I should string him up instead. What d'ya reckon, gal?'

'There's not a tree worthy of a rope in sight, honey.'

'That's true.'

'Besides, I've gotten used to the idea of blowing his head off. In fact I'm looking forward to it.'

Ryan thought: What kind of demon had Cuskin loosed in Belle Boothley's heart and soul to change her from schoolmarm to killer?

'His blood will bond us for ever, Frank,' she said breathlessly.

'For ever aren't words that Cuskin understands, Belle,' Abe Ryan said. 'He'll dump you for the next skirt that gets his blood up.'

'No he won't!' Belle raged. A sudden and awful fear took her over. 'You never would, would you, Frank?'

'Can't you see what he's tryin' to do, Belle?' Cuskin scoffed. 'Turn ya agin me with lies.'

'You know deep down, Belle, that what I say is true,' Ryan said.

An even sharper fear gripped Belle Boothley. Her eyes darted between the outlaw and the marshal, her confusion and doubt stark. Ryan could see that the scales were finely balanced between acceptance of his assertion and Cuskin's assurance, and could tip either way in the next couple of seconds.

Belle Boothley was holding a cocked pistol which could be swayed either way, a fact that Frank Cuskin was suddenly and keenly aware of.

'If you have nothing to say, Frank, then maybe Marshal Ryan is right in what he's said will happen.'

With the cunning learned over many years of mayhem and murder, the outlaw turned the tables again.

'If you believe that, Belle, darlin', then use that gun on me. 'Cause you doubtin' my love for ya, makes me wanna die an'way.'

With the gullibility of a fool wanting to believe, Belle Boothley's eyes glowed again with the fire of passion and desire. She focused the wavering gun on Ryan.

'Right between the eyes, Frank.'

'That's my gal.'

In the seconds before he died, Abe Ryan had an ocean of regrets about what he might have done and what he had neglected to do, and top of his list of regrets was the fact that he had squandered his chance to be with Kate Collins, always figuring when he got cold feet that there would be tomorrow to try again, ignoring the reality that one day, like now, would cancel tomorrow. He thought about prayer, but wasn't sure that the God he had stopped talking to so long ago would welcome his return, now that hell's fire was licking his boots.

But maybe he was judging God by man's standards.

He heard the Lord's Prayer running through his head, the way it had done when he was a kid and alone in the dark. God had listened then. So he might listen again. The man had come a long and sinful way from the boy, but if he was to believe his ma and pa, good folk that they had been, God was always listening, always welcoming, and always forgiving.

'What the hell're ya waitin' for, Belle?' Cuskin growled.

Frank Cuskin's snarl got Abe Ryan's full attention. He looked to Belle Boothley, and saw her troubled look. The gun in her hand was shaking.

She could not pull the trigger!

The decent woman deep inside Belle Boothley came to the fore.

'I can't do it,' she said. 'I've already killed Doc Murray for you, Frank. And that was wrong, too. I've damned my immortal soul for you, Frank.'

'Then you can't damn it twice, can ya. So dispatch the marshal!'

'Ain't easy to kill a man in cold blood, is it, Belle?' Ryan said. 'That's much to your credit.'

'Stop the palaver, Ryan,' Cuskin barked. 'Ain't goin' to do you no good.'

'Can't we just leave him be?' Belle Boothley pleaded. 'He's as good as done for anyway.'

'I ain't gonna take no chances,' the outlaw growled. 'He found me once. I don't want to see his ugly face in my shavin' mirror some mornin'.' He grabbed the gun from Belle Boothley. 'I'll shoot the bastard myself.' Then cocked and ready, Cuskin eased back the hammer of the six-gun, grinned evilly. 'Too quick,' he said. 'Ya know, Belle,

74

that idea you had about hogtying the marshal and leaving him for the hungry critters hereabouts to feed on him kinda appeals to me more than dispatchin' him fast with a bullet in his skull.'

Belle Boothley paled.

'You seem to be gone right off that plan, Belle.'

'I spoke out of turn, Frank. Look,' she cuddled up to Cuskin, 'why don't we take his horse and leave him be. Without a horse there's no way out of this hellhole.'

Cuskin shoved her away from him.

'Don't know what's got into ya, Belle.,But you're turnin' out to be a real disappointment to me, gal.'

'The marshal is right, isn't he? You'll leave me high and dry the first chance you get.'

'Ain't so, Belle.' Cuskin turned on his considerable charm again. 'You're my woman, always will be.'

The light of hope renewed shone in Belle Boothley's eyes. 'Ya gotta understand, honey. This bastard would have strung me up if you hadn't happened along. So that makes me real angry with him. Ya can understand that, can't ya?'

'Sure I can, Frank,' she said breathlessly, as once more Cuskin pressed her against him, her fleeting resolve (much to Ryan's despair) to challenge the outlaw now going up in smoke.

'And ya wouldn't want this lawdog to survive and

keep lookin' for me, now would ya?'

'No.'

'That's my gal.' Cuskin added kiss to clinch, and when he broke away Belle Boothley was more lost a soul than she had ever been. He handed her the six-gun. 'Now, you keep that aimed right at the marshal's heart, honey, while I hogtie him to the wagon wheel. And if he as much as blinks an eye, shoot him.'

When Ryan was secured and helpless Cuskin was greatly pleased. He stood over Ryan and kicked him mercilessly on the side of the head. As punishment was added to punishment Ryan retched. What little strength he had drained away, leaving him limp, vowing that one day he would again track and snare Cuskin. Only next time he might not be of a mind to apply the rules of gentlemanly conduct or honest law.

But in his heart of hearts he knew that Cuskin had won.

Cuskin drew Belle Boothley to him, 'Ya know Belle, seein' the marshal all trussed up and in a sorry state makes me feel quite lovin',' he whispered in her ear. Her eyes popped. 'Thought you'd like the idea,' he laughed. 'Got a plan, honey. We can ride on come mornin', about an hour 'fore dawn. We'll put out the fire to invite those hungry desert critters in. A hour should be plenty of time for them to feast on the marshal. But for now,' he grabbed Boothley roughly by the hair and kissed her violently, 'I figger some lovin' is my due, Belle.'

As good as his word, Frank Cuskin was ready to ride an hour before dawn. He checked the rawhide binding with which he had bound the Bewley marshal. 'Wouldn't want ya slippin' those knots, Ryan.' Satisfied with his handiwork, Cuskin returned to Belle Boothley, who was as pleased as a cat after cream following the hours she had spent with Cuskin. 'Happy?' the outlaw enquired of her.

'Over the moon, honey,' she answered with a sigh.

'Good. Let's ride, gal.'

With the giddiness of a young girl, Belle Boothley went to mount up. Abe Ryan called out a warning to her, but Cuskin acted with the swiftness of a mountain cat. The blow of the rock on Boothley's skull, was gut-wrenching. Belle Boothley swung around slowly, blood obscenely matting her mane of fair hair from the gash on her head.

'So the marshal was right, Frank,' she said mournfully.

He sneered.

'Should have listened, I guess, Belle. Try to

77

understand, honey. I move real fast. So a woman along would slow me up somethin' awful. Now, a skirt I can get any time. So why have the bother of havin' one along.'

He struck her again with the bloodied rock.

The blow sent Belle Boothley staggering back like a Saturday-night drunk. Then, for a split second she held her ground and straightened up proudly defiant, before folding.

Untroubled, in fact seeming quite pleased, Frank Cuskin kicked dirt on the fire, then mounted up. 'Ya know, Ryan, I'm surely pleased the way things have worked out. I guess ya ain't so pleased though.' He glanced down with utter disdain at Belle Boothley. 'All that fresh blood will have hungry critters all over ya in no time at all, Marshal. *Adios.* See ya in hell, Ryan.'

'I'll come lookin' for you, Cuskin,' Ryan promised feebly.

'I ain't goin' to be troubled by no ghost, Ryan,' he scoffed ' 'Cause ghosts can't shoot.'

Laughing, Cuskin rode away, unconcerned that he had murdered one human being and had left another to face certain death.

As he had said, the scent of fresh blood would lure predators. And, cunning as they were, Abe Ryan knew that it would not take them long to realize that he was helpless to fight them off. Once that happened they would come in their droves to rip him apart. And if, against all the odds, he survived until sunup, his death would be slower and all the more torturous as he fried in the desert heat, waiting for the buzzards to tear at him as soon as he passed out, or maybe even before. He strained manfully against his binding, but there was not even a smidgen of give. His spirits never lower, Abe Ryan reckoned that it would be best if death came quickly to him.

It was not long before eyes flashed and jaws gnashed in the half-light between night and morning. A coyote put in an appearance, like a shy kid at a party hanging round the edges, trying to work up the courage to become involved. Abe Ryan's thrashing about put a stopper on him. A second predator joined the first. Its eyes flashed between the thrashing Ryan and the still Boothley. Its decision was an easy one to make.

Belle Boothley.

Taking courage, more appeared.

Abe Ryan's stomach heaved at the thought of what would happen in the next couple of minutes. But at least Belle Boothley was dead.

Trussed up, he'd be devoured alive!

CHAPTER SEVEN

About to feast, the coyotes were suddenly put to flight when Belle Boothley rolled over on her back and waved her hands in the air. Her gesture was a feeble one but, startled, the coyotes vanished back into the half-light to regroup.

Ryan, as startled as the coyotes, called out, 'I thought you were dead, Belle.'

She sat up slowly, the crusting of dried blood on her face making her a fearsome sight. She began to crawl forward, every inch gained heaping agony on agony, pain on pain. 'There's a Bowie hidden under the wagon seat. If I can make it.'

'Let it be,' Ryan said. 'Save your strength, Belle.'

'I'm already as good as dead. It's a downright miracle that I've come to. I've done terrible wrong, Marshal. I want to set the record to rights before I meet my Maker. If I can cut you loose, I'll have gone some way to make amends. So don't try and stop me. Because I want to stop so much.'

Abe Ryan knew the truth of what she'd said. There was no hope for Belle Boothley. Again, she began her slow, torturous crawl, each inch gained taking her closer to death. The gap to bridge was not great, but having to claw at it inch by terrible inch with the Grim Reaper on your back made for a long journey. One which, Ryan reckoned, Belle Boothley would not complete.

As the seconds ticked by, the Bewley marshal began to pray that Belle Boothley would let go. If it was God's forgiveness and friendship she was seeking, he figured that she had earned them a hundred times over.

Slowly, and slower still, Belle Boothley made progress until she was pulling herself up the wagon with a grim determination. She reached under the seat, but toppled back on to the rocky ground, adding pain to pain.

She curled up in a ball and went still.

'Thanks for trying, Belle,' Ryan said quietly. 'I hope the hereafter is all you wanted it to be.'

'I'm not there yet to find out, Marshal,' she croaked.

When Belle Boothley once more began to claw herself up the wagon, Abe Ryan reckoned that he was indeed witness to a miracle. This time, steadying herself as best she could, her hand reappeared from under the wagon seat, holding the precious Bowie. But would she have the strength left to use it?

She dropped on to her knees alongside Ryan, rolled under the wagon, and began her attempt to cut through the rawhide binding that secured the marshal to the wagon wheel. Her breath was ragged, and death rattled in her throat, but she kept cutting, her efforts getting more feeble by the second.

The coyotes were back. But instead of two, there were five.

The Bowie clattered to the ground. The stomach-churning sound of Belle Boothley's death rattles filled the air. Belle whimpered, the way a body does when the fight is lost.

More predators arrived.

Abe Ryan knew that any second now they would be all over him, powerful jaws ripping his flesh from his bones. He strained on his bindings, but they still held firm. Frustrated, a great anger took him over and he tried again.

The binding snapped. His hands came free. He stood up on legs rendered near useless by the lack of circulation. But now that Belle Boothley had worked her miracle, he was not going to see it wasted. With a towering rage, he began battering the ravenous horde with rocks, shouting: 'If you want me, you're going to have to fight to get me!' Confused, the creatures milled about for a while, before a hefty rock landed on one of them and, howling, it turned tail. Sensing harm, and a meal lost, the others also fled.

Abe Ryan collapsed, spent, on to the ground. The coming day was tingeing the rim of the night sky. In no time at all dawn would break.

On a day Abe Ryan had never expected to see.

He lay for a spell, the sun spinning and weaving a thousand colours in sky and desert. He waited patiently for his hurting body to recover as best it could. He had another grave to ready. Belle Boothley the schoolmarm, would never have expected to lie in death in the rough burial place in which she would now rest, and he could only wonder what spell Frank Cuskin had weaved for her to become his woman. Maybe the lure of evil was more exciting than the quietude of respectability.

Whatever, Abe Ryan felt a deep pity for Belle Boothley.

He rolled over, hoping that he had enough strength in his hands and arms to get him upright. That was when he spotted what he hoped was not a mirage that would cruelly vanish when he reached for it.

Slowly, expecting the rawhide waterbag secreted away under the wagon to vanish at his touch, Ryan reached out, and was filled with a heady excitement on feeling the plump, pliable coolness of the skin between his fingers. Doc Murray had been a savvy man. If trouble came a-calling, the precious contents of the water barrel in a drought-plagued land could be more valuable than any gold or goods. So he had planned ahead by rigging a waterbag as reserve. Ryan's urge was to grab the bag from the hooks on which it hung and guzzle from it, but wiser counsel prevailed. Grasping fingers might puncture it.

Gingerly, he levered the waterskin free, cradling it in his arms with the gentleness of a mother holding her newborn babe. He uncorked the skin. Water spilled over the lip of the opening, and he almost grabbed at the opening to stop each precious drop from being wasted, but had he done so the bag might have slid from his grasp and most of the water would have been lost to the arid ground. The shock of the mistake he had almost made, sent shivers as cold as Yukon ice through him.

Steadying himself, Ryan raised the waterbag and drank, revelling in the sting of his cracked lips as the precious balm dribbled into his mouth and down his parched throat. He wanted to drink every drop of water, but forced himself to consume it slowly, letting his dried innards become accustomed to what they had lacked, and not be overcome by the shock of relief. He leaned back against the wagon, feeling the tightness leave his innards, sending stabs of pain into his deepest parts, until they too became acclimatized to the bliss of hydration. The muscles and tendons became unknotted, letting strength back into them.

The water brought a hunger, too, but his craving for food came second to his need for refreshment. He was ready to stand up. Using the wagon as support, until he felt confident enough to let go of it as a prop, he exercised and massaged his cramped legs until the circulation returned. He paced back and forth, feeling his limbs gather strength and energy, until he felt capable of, and energetic enough, to dance an Irish jig. Renewed, Ryan searched the wagon for grub, and was amply rewarded with jerky, beans, coffee, and some rye bread.

But before he grubbed, he would show due respect to Belle Boothley and plant her as best he could. He took her lifeless body in his arms and carried her to a shallow dip in the ground which would serve as a grave of sorts. And, as he had done before with Doc Murray, he covered her with rocks.

'Ain't a fitting burial, Belle,' he said. 'But it's all there is out here.' He said a few words to a God whom he had come to appreciate more than he had done for a heck of a long time.

Then, respects paid, he started a fire and began to prepare his first meal for days. Better still, he would be able to wash it down with coffee made with fresh water.

Breakfast over, Abe Ryan began to think about Frank Cuskin. Having witnessed his brutality and cruelty at first hand, he felt a steely resolve to hunt him down building in him. However, his horse wasn't up to much. He doubted that the mare would have the grit to carry him far, let alone catch up Cuskin with the head start the outlaw had.

Another problem was Cuskin's knowledge of the desert and its highways and byways, a knowledge that Ryan could not match. There were trails, but he doubted very much if Cuskin would choose to travel by routes that most folk used; no, sir, he'd use the owlhoot passages where help from his kind would be readily forthcoming were he to have his tail dogged. If he had any advantage, it was, Abe Ryan reckoned, that Cuskin would not have counted on him still being alive, let alone kicking.

'I'm going to be asking a hell of a lot from you,' Ryan coaxed the mare. 'Do your best, gal. Can't ask for more.'

He filled a tin washbasin that he found among Doc Murray's cooking utensils with water. The mare drank it greedily. She'd have gladly consumed every drop of the water in the waterbag but, not knowing when he'd cross paths again with Cuskin (if ever), Ryan could not afford to be any more generous than he had been.

Ready to make tracks, Ryan returned to Belle Boothley's makeshift resting place to say a final few words of prayer and thanks.

'If I can, Belle, I'll take revenge for what Cuskin did to you out of his hide,' he promised.

Ryan had his leg in the stirrup when he sensed someone behind him. First thoughts were that Frank Cuskin had had a premonition and had turned back. Or that his seeking kin had arrived. Ryan had to work an advantage if he could, so he swung into the saddle as if he hadn't a care in the world.

'Easy, gal,' he soothed the mare when the horse took exception to a rider on its exhausted back. Having settled the horse down, he made as though to ride away, but instead he threw himself clear of the saddle, six-gun already in his mitt before he came to crouch on the ground. But, canny as he had been, he found himself looking down the barrel of a Winchester rifle. The man holding the rifle said, in a manner that made it clear that he'd pull the trigger without qualm:

'Drop the iron and come up slow, hands high.'

CHAPTER EIGHT

'Abe,' the man said, when Ryan came upright to face his menacer, an unmistakable note of surprise in his voice.

Ryan shaded his eyes against the glare of the sun, and instantly recognized Henry Bowdrie. 'Why the hell are you pointing that thing at me, Henry?' the marshal growled.

Bowdrie reacted in the manner of a man who had right on his side.

'What did you expect. All I seen was a fella plantin' a woman.'

'I'm a lawman,' Ryan barked. 'And you don't point weapons at a lawman!'

'Far as I was concerned, you were just a murdering coyote, Abe. And if you was me, you'd have done 'xactly the same. And don't say you wouldn't!'

Bowdrie's logic took the steam out of Ryan's grouse.

'I guess, Henry,' he said.

'Near didn't find you neither,' Bowdrie griped. 'With you going every which way, like the snapped elastic of a woman's drawers.'

'Find me?'

'Yeah. Find you. Ain't that what I just said?'

'Find me, means you were looking for me.'

'Ain't you a real cleverclogs, Marshal Ryan.'

'A deal?' Ryan grumbled.

'A deal,' Bowdrie agreed.

'Let's stop all of this horseshit, and you tell me why you came looking for me?'

'Simple to understand, even for a hole-in-the-head, mule-stubborn cuss like you, Abe.'

'Thought we had a deal,' Ryan barked.

'We have.'

'Then have the good grace to honour it, Bowdrie.'

Henry Bowdrie swept the battered, sweat stained hat from his head, bald except for a couple of strands of shock-red hair, which he scratched.

'Kate hired me to come find ya.'

'Kate? You mean Kate Collins?'

'That Kate, yeah. Give me a hundred dollars, she said, if I fetched ya back to Bewley.' Bowdrie grinned toothlessly. 'Real sweet on you, Kate is.'

He shook his head in wonder. 'No understandin' women, is there? That gal could have any man in Bewley, and a whole lot of other places too. Men with deep pockets that would keep her like she should be kept, like one of them fancy European princesses. And she's gone and fallen for you. Like I said, there ain't no understandin' women.'

Bowdrie rolled his huge eyes to emphasize his lack of understanding. They were the eyes of a black man. His tendrils of red hair showed the Irish in him, and his slanted features were Indian, probably Apache.

Henry Bowdrie was a man of mixed influences.

Marshal Abe Ryan scowled.

'Can I now ask what I've tried to ask five times since you started gabbing, Bowdrie?'

'Ya know, Marshal Ryan. Anyone ever tell you that you're as sweet-natured as a viper 'bout to bite ya on the ass!'

Ryan looked to the sky. 'Right now I'm needing a passel of patience, Lord. And if you don't give it to me, I'll damn my soul by murdering this crotchety old-timer.'

'Old-timer?' Bowdrie yelped. 'For two bits, I'd whup you, lawman or no lawman!'

Ryan grabbed Bowdrie by the shirt and hauled him face to face. 'Are you telling me that Kate Collins was so worried about my welfare that she gave you one hundred dollars to come and get me, Bowdrie?'

'Ain't that what I've been tellin' ya, Abe?' Bowdrie groaned. 'On fetchin' ya back to her. And you'd have heard me too, if your mouth gave your ears a chance.'

'You know,' Ryan chuckled, 'you've got me fair worn out, Henry.'

'No I ain't. Your present mood ain't got nothin' to do with being worn out. You've got love sickness, plain as the nose on your face. 'Cause the second it clicked with you that Kate Collins wanted you back safe and sound to Bewley, and her lovin' arms around you, the salty sass went right outta ya.'

Henry Bowdrie sighed with a deep satisfaction. 'If it was me she wanted back I'd be leapin' right over that sun right now.'

Abe Ryan laughed. 'Henry. . . .'

'Yeah.' Henry's sigh was all the deeper.

'You got the look of a man with dreams you shouldn't be having,' Ryan said good humouredly.

'Heck, Abe, dreamin' is all a man can do, when a man can't do, if you get my drift.'

Their shared laughter was that of good friends.

Henry Bowdrie and Abe Ryan had first met up fifteen years previously when Bowdrie was an army scout, and Ryan had earned his crust as a wrangler on the Golden Eagle spread, owned by a fella called Dan Mooney, as hard-as-nails a boss as any man could work for. Mean and nasty, that was Mooney; a man so stingy with a cup of water and mean with a dime that he gave skinflints a good name.

Bowdrie was the exception to such treatment. He was always welcome and treated regally, due to the fact that years before he had rescued Mooney's wife from the clutches of four Apache bucks intent on having their way before they scalped Mary Mooney's mane of golden hair. Mooney was Irish. Bowdrie had had flowing red locks at that time, which told Mooney that somewhere along the line an Irishman had planted his seed. Both sets of circumstances made Bowdrie, as far as Dan Mooney was concerned, a man among men, always welcome to visit or stay over for as long as it pleased him to do so at the Golden Eagle.

Both Mary and Dan Mooney had now shucked the mortal coil, Dan to a bull who was as mean as he was, and Mary to fever. However, Andy Mooney, Dan and Mary's son, had lived up to the promise he'd made his pa on his deathbed, to make Henry Bowdrie welcome whenever he dropped by.

Abe Ryan had made Bowdrie's acquaintance on his first visit to the Golden Eagle. It was an acquaintance that grew into friendship; a friendship which had grown in warmth despite the passing of time in which their paths had less and less frequently crossed. In fact it had been almost five years since Abe Ryan had set eyes on Bowdrie before he arrived in Bewley the day Cuskin committed murder and, allowing for the shedding of his hair and a couple of extra wrinkles round his eyes, he had not changed. He was not a young man by Western standards; he was long past riding the lonely and dangerous trails of desert and wilderness. But it looked like he had meant what he'd said a long time ago: that when his time came he wanted to see a sky full of stars and feel a gentle breeze on his face.

Bowdrie had long since given up on being an army scout, but not on scouting. Nowadays he hired out, sometimes as an escort, sometimes as a wagonmaster, and other times, when no one was hiring, he simply took to the trails and lived life by his motto of 'come what may'. It was not a life that suited every man, including Ryan himself. But it was one heck of a free life for the man who could take each day and what that day brought in his stride.

'Roots and walls make me real jittery,' he had once confided to Ryan. Henry Bowdrie was truly a man of nature in its rawest and often its roughest sense.

'Like to tell me what happened here?' Bowdrie enquired of the Bewley lawman.

'The woman buried under that pile of stones is a woman called Belle Boothley, Henry. Frank Cuskin's woman. Or so she thought, before he cracked her skull when her usefulness was done with.' Ryan went on to tell Bowdrie the full story, and as it unfolded Bowdrie's astonishment intensified. 'Now, I know that you reckon that I was suckered good and proper in a manner that ain't fitting for a lawman to be.'

'You got that right,' Bowdrie said, deadpan.

'But that's how it was. And if you tell another soul, I'll forget that I'm a badge-toter and cut your heart out! Understood?'

'That's as clear as you can make it, I guess, Abe,' Bowdrie said.

'Furthermore, if you don't wipe that grin from your face, I'll shove it right down your throat! Now that you've found me, you go straight back to Bewley and tell Kate Collins that I ain't no wet-behind-the-ears kid who needs finding!'

'Got it. Only one thing, Abe. . . .'

'And that is?'

'You might blow your chances with Kate, and that would be real dumb of ya. She said to me, word for word now. Mr Bowdrie, sir, she's got respect—'

'For age.'

'You're a barrel of laughs, ain't ya, Abe Ryan?'

'Kate said?'

'Dunno if I'll tell ya now. But I guess it wouldn't be fair to Kate. She said: "Mr Bowdrie, sir. You go find and bring back that mule-headed cuss Abe Ryan, who I just happen to love the pants off".'

'Kate said that?'

'Didn't I just tell ya she did? Must be all this desert dust cloggin' your ears. Now if I tell Kate that I ran you to ground, then left you where you was, she's liable to up and blow a hole right through me. Now, I ask you, Abe. Would you be able to sleep nights if that happened?'

'Hearing it like you've told it, it surely is hard not to head back,' Ryan said. 'But I have a job to do, Henry, and that's to haul Frank Cuskin back to Bewley to be hanged. And if I don't do that, then I surely won't be able to sleep a wink, thinkng about all those other folk Cuskin will murder, because I didn't do what my badge says I should have done. You go tell Kate Collins what I said. She'll understand.'

'Can't you get it through that thick skull of yours?' Bowdrie argued. 'Kate Collins is sprouting grey hairs by the second, frettin' that she'll never set eyes on you again, Abe. Now you can relieve that gal's awful sufferin' right now by headin' back to Bewley. Once there, with Kate and you cosied up to each other, you can raise a posse to round up the whole bunch of Cuskins. I'll even help ya, Abe.'

'I know that, you old bastard,' Ryan said warmly.

'Havin' me along will make all the diff'rence, I reckon.'

'Big-headed, ain't you!'

'I'm the best scout round these parts by a long shot, Abe.' Ryan knew that was the truth of it. 'It makes a man secure in the saddle, knowin' that someone's along who knows what he's doin'. Don't mean to insult ya none, Abe. . . .'

'That a fact?' Ryan said drily.

'But facts is facts, and there's no changin' that.'

'Are you done?' Ryan asked tersely.

'Done,' Bowdrie said. 'Like it or not.'

'Now get this through that shiny dome of yours, Henry. I'll only say it once. . . .'

'I reckon once will be enough.'

'If I have to wander around this god-forsaken desert for the rest of my natural, or have my bones bleaching in the sun, I ain't going back to Bewley without Frank Cuskin in tow. You tell Kate what I've said, and take no blame on yourself. Tell her also to give you the hundred dollars she's promised, and if she thinks the giving of it wasn't justified, tell her that when I get back I'll make good the hundred to the cent.'

'If you make it back, don't ya mean? Forget the

97

hundred dollars, Abe. Don't count none. I'd have come after ya for nothin'. Goin' after Cuskin on your ownsome was loco to start with. And goin' after him now is even more loco.'

'I don't disagree,' Ryan said. 'But it's what I've got to do, Henry.'

'Even if it means that Kate Collins is a widder 'fore she even ties the knot, Abe?'

'You can't be a widow before you tie the knot, Henry.'

'Don't smart talk me, Abe Ryan. If you don't come back, Kate, pinin' for ya the way she is, will be a widder in her heart 'til the day she dies, and spoiled for any other man. Is that what you want?'

'No it ain't, Henry,' Ryan said sincerely. 'But what kind of man would Kate be getting if I didn't live up to the oath I swore the day I pinned on a lawman's badge.' Shaking his head, the Bewley marshal put up his hand to stall Bowdrie's protestations. 'I'm going to bring Frank Cuskin to book for Dan Cleary's murder. Whatever the cost, Henry.'

Henry Bowdrie shuffled, trying to find a way back into the argument which Abe Ryan had resolutely closed. Finding none, he said, 'Well, if that's an end of it, I guess we'd better hit the trail 'fore Cuskin can make it all the way to Mexico. I ain't a picky sorta fella, Abe. But I have to admit to not likin' Mexes much.'

'Mexicans are no better or worse than anyone else, Henry. Good and bad in all sorts and all kinds. And you not likin' Mexes won't enter in to it. Because I'm going on alone.'

'Alone!'

'That's what I said, Henry. A-L-O-N-E, *amigo.*'

'I've met some mule-stubborn critters in my time, Abe Ryan. But I can tell ya that you're the biggest mule's rear end yet.'

'And don't follow, neither,' Ryan warned.

'Can I give a pointer?'

'That I'd welcome, Henry.'

'I guess it's somethin'. Kate will skin me alive when she'll see me ridin' into Bewley without you.'

'You don't have to tell her that you found me.'

'I ain't and never have been a lyin' man, Abe Ryan. And I don't aim to start now.'

'The pointer?'

'Yeah. The pointer,' Bowdrie said resignedly. 'South of here, ten miles, maybe a little more, you'll come to a string of slapped-together shacks that folk who hang 'round there call a town. Ain't got no name. No one ever thought it worth namin'. It's nothin' more than a liquor stop for Cuskin's kind, before they ride on to Mexico, or a roost 'bout a mile east called Hannigan's Reach. I figger that that's where Cuskin headed when he left you and the woman for gonners. There he can rest 'mong his own kind, 'fore he cuts the next trail. Hannigan's Reach has got moonshine and women, and a man like Frank Cuskin don't need no more.'

'Thanks, Henry.'

'You won't be thankin' me any when Hannigan and his bunch of henchemen will take ya to the top of the Reach and sling you into the gorge below, all of a hundred-foot drop. That's, of course, if you ever get to leave the shack town. To the men there, a lawman's scent is as ripe as a coyote's.'

'I've been in plenty of tight spots before, Henry. I can be a pretty good actor when needs be.'

'Even if you get outta the shack town, and outta Hannigan's Reach with Cuskin your prisoner, you'll still have a heck of a journey back to Bewley, Abe.' The shake of Henry Bowdrie's head graphically conveyed to Ryan the improbability, in his opinion, of the Bewley marshal completing the task he'd set himself. Bowdrie's next statement bluntly removed any chance of Ryan not getting the message. 'Talkin' no bullshit, if you do this on your ownsome, I figger that you're as good as dead right now, Abe.'

Bowdrie's assessment was not one with which Abe Ryan could honestly disagree. However, his determination to see Frank Cuskin swing, now above all else for Belle Boothley's murder, was all the stronger.

'If you'll just let me tag along outta sight, Abe,' Bowdrie pleaded. 'I can move like a ghost in these parts. No one will know I'm tailin' ya.'

'I'll know, Henry. And knowing will only add to my concerns.'

'What concerns would they be?'

'That you'll catch an arrow, or lead.'

'I've been dodgin' both for longer than I can remember, Abe.'

'All the more reason I don't want your luck running out nursemaiding me, Henry.'

'Never took too kindly to help, did ya?'

'I guess not,' Ryan admitted.

'Always want to go your own way, and do things your own way?'

'I guess that about says it, Henry.'

'Ya know what, Abe Ryan. . . ?'

'What?'

'I'm sure goin' to enjoy watchin' Kate Collins clip your wings.'

The Bewley marshal chuckled. 'You know, Henry, if there's one to do it, I reckon Kate's that one. But. . . .'

'But what?'

'It'll be because I'll like her doing it, Henry.'

Henry Bowdrie took on a dreamy look. 'Heck, Abe. I figger that you'll like her doin' a whole bundle to ya.'

'Go back to Bewley, Henry. Tell Kate I'll be calling on her one day soon to be my wife.'

Bowdrie's high spirits of a moment before drooped.

'I'll pray that you'll make it back, Abe,' he said sincerely.

'And I surely hope that you'll be listened to, Henry.'

'That nag you're on ain't up to much. Take mine, Abe. I'll have time to nurse yours along.'

Abe Ryan mounted up.

'My lot is my lot, Henry. And my doing is my doing. I don't want anyone else to pay a price for my foolishness.'

'You could try Mame Benteen's along the way. She's a cunning old witch who'll take the eye out of your head if you let her. But she's been known to have one or two good horses to trade from time to time.'

'And where do I find Mame Benteen?' Ryan enquired.

Bowdrie pointed. 'A coupla miles. Can't miss Mame's. Flies her drawers off a mast to stop the buzzards pickin' at the horseflesh and her when she's skunk drunk.' Bowdrie laughed. 'Works, too.

You'll see why when you see Mame Benteen's drawers flappin' in the wind.'

Ryan's hope of a fresh horse took a dive when he saw the direction in which Bowdrie had pointed. It was where he had seen smoke rise from.

'See any Indians on your travels, Henry?'

Bowdrie shook his head.

'Been no Indian trouble for a long spell now, Abe. Of course that don't say that there won't be again.'

'You take care, Henry.'

'You too, Abe,' Bowdrie repeated worriedly as he watched Ryan ride away. He thought about giving Ryan a head start, then doing as he'd suggested and tagging along. But he'd risk Ryan spotting him. And if he did, it would be the end of a friendship which Bowdrie cherished dearly.

'God go with you, Abe.' Henry Bowdrie mounted up and headed back to Bewley.

CHAPTER NINE

Conscious of the distance Frank Cuskin had opened up on him, Abe Ryan had an urge to make tracks, but he wisely opted for a more moderate pace. The mare was game, but her legs wobbled a time or two, and to be thrown on to the rocky terrain over which he was travelling could cause a bone-breaking injury, even fatality. In the desert country injury and death would most likely be partners. At least now, thanks to Belle Boothley, he was sucking air and had grub and water, which put him in a lot better shape than he had previously been.

Ryan knew that in the desert nothing could be taken for granted, danger was never far away. But momentarily he forgot how close it could really be until a pair of Apache bucks materialized as if by magic up ahead of him. That was the thing about the Apache: masters of stealth, you did not see them until they wanted to be seen. No white man could match an Indian in trickery. Sometimes they were just curious, the way a white man might be on finding an intruder in his backyard. Or they might be in a mood for trading. Other times their presence was far more menacing.

In recent times the Apache had mostly been peaceful, but peace between the white man and the Indian was a day-to-day affair, with hostilities never far below the surface. Trouble could come spit quick, due to malicious intent or sheer stupidity by either side, and peace went up like smoke from a bottle and vanished as quickly.

Ryan came up short and waited for a sign as to the Indians' intentions, hoping that the pair were alone and (conscious of the smoke he had seen) not part of a war party. As the stand-off lengthened, Ryan wished that he knew Apache lingo to explain his presence. Or that they had white man's tongue to ask what questions they needed to ask.

'I come in peace,' was all Ryan could say, and he said it in a manner that he hoped would convince the Indians of the veracity of his statement. The response to his declaration was excited chatter between the Apache bucks.

Their chatter ceased.

Ryan tensed.

Waited.

His heart beat a rapid tattoo.

Knowing that the slightest change in body posture would be seen as threatening, Abe Ryan sat unmoving in the saddle, conscious that his static state would leave him ill-prepared, should the Indians attack.

Circling vultures swooped low. Ryan had his answer. Swooping vultures was a portent of blood-letting. One of the Apaches had a repeater rifle. His partner had only bow and arrow and a hunting blade in his waistband. It was only a matter of seconds between the buzzards' appearance and gunplay. Like Ryan, the bucks took their cue from the vultures.

Ryan ducked low in the saddle as an arrow whizzed overhead, nicking the top of his left ear in passing. Blood ran down his left cheek into the hollow of his neck. He had the Winchester free of its saddle scabbard and levelled at the Indian bearing the rifle. In his experience, Apaches were not great marksmen, but his experience was a time ago, and by now they could have learned the art of straight shooting rather than random lead-slinging.

Deciding that the rifleman was the more lethal (though the bow-and-arrow Apache had shown his prowess), Abe Ryan fired at the gun-toting Indian on the basis that lead travelled faster than an arrow. The buck reared up, clutching his chest, trying desperately to stem the flow of blood from the Winchester's bullet hole.

His agony was short-lived. The second Apache, used to death all round him, wasted no sympathy on his partner; his only purpose now was to lay low the white man who had brought about the death of a fellow Indian. Ryan cut loose again at the charging buck, but the Apache's weaving approach left little if any chance of nailing him. A third shot was not on. The buck was upon him, hunting blade reflecting the sunlight, as he leaped from his pony to grapple with Ryan, bringing them both crashing to the ground.

With the expertise and agility for which the Apache were known, the Indian had the knife to Abe Ryan's throat on landing, but fortunately for him the Indian's angle was too acute to enable him to use the blade swiftly and needed readjustment. Ryan drove an elbow hard into the Indian's belly. The Apache soaked up its punishment in stomach muscle made firm by a lifetime of hard, often gruelling work. The Apache spun. The blade of the hunting knife licked Ryan's Adam's apple, ready to open his throat. Ryan slipped the Indian's hold, and slung a handful of dust in the Apache's face. He used the Indian's second of blindness to swing a boot into his groin.

The Indian let loose a tormented howl that scattered the buzzards already tearing at the downed Apache. One of the evil birds, flying over Ryan, dropped his tasty morsel – an eye. It bounced along the ground. A second, more daring buzzard, now one of a whole passel of the vile creatures, swooped and snatched up the eye.

A second kick to the ribs sent the Apache spinning. He fell face down, and gave a grunt before going still. When Ryan turned him over, the hunting blade was up to the hilt in his gut.

Conscious that the bucks might have been scouts for a larger party of Apaches, Ryan waited and listened. And prayed, too. There was nothing he could do if his fears were confirmed. The seconds lengthened into minutes. The minutes mounted to ten with slow torture. Nothing happened. He waited a little more, before making a move. Slowly, eyes scanning, Abe Ryan got to his feet, half-expecting an arrow or gunshot to bring him down. Neither came. Gradually, realizing that he was alone, except for the feeding vultures, he began to breathe easy, reckoning that, like the cat, he had nine lives.

Lives that he was using up fast.

It was near to sunset when he eventually reached

what had been Mame Benteen's horse ranch, not that it had been much of a ranch as far as he could tell, just a shack and a corral. The shack was a smouldering ruin, the corral was empty. The only sign that Mame Benteen had ever existed was a scatter of torn bloodstained female apparel, which Abe Ryan took as evidence that the woman had not only been slaughtered, but that her death had come after she had suffered violation.

Ryan found Mame Benteen lying naked, dumped in a nearby gully. She had not been scalped. Neither could he find any other sign of Indians, which made Ryan wonder if she had been the victim of an Apache attack at all. White men, of the Cuskin kind, had previously raped and pillaged and placed the blame for their misdeeds on the Indian. Apaches were no saints, but they were not always the sinners mythology would have you believe.

Ryan found a spade back of the burned-out shack. He scooped a dozen shovels of sandy soil over Mame Benteen. It was only a gesture. By dawn of the next day there would be little of Mame Benteen's mortal remains left – even her bones would have been carted off to chew on.

'Nothing but bodies to bury, hoss,' Ryan said bitterly. As he rode away (at crawling pace now, the mare was so exhausted) he made himself a promise that if he survived, he would grow old with Kate Collins in Bewley.

The evening had grown progressively darker and heavy with the lack of air. Ryan looked to the stormheads rolling up from Mexico, marching across the sky like the vanguard soldiers of a conqueror, and there was no greater conqueror than Mother Nature. He welcomed the cooling balm of the freshening breeze being pushed ahead of the storm. However, the breeze and the cooling rain spatters were the deceptive forerunners of a desert storm that could bring more problems than it solved. Gullies and draws would fill and becoming raging torrents. Trails would vanish under mudslides and change the topography of the country. Lightning would become a fiery agent of death.

Abe Ryan hoped that, by the time the storm broke in its full and terrible intensity, he would have reached the shack town Henry Bowdrie had spoken of. Because if he had not, the game of survival, the tussle between him and the desert, would become all the more challenging.

The wind was picking up, and the rain spatters were beginning to join together in a more substantial downpour.

An hour later, in the full teeth of the storm, it was looking as though the desert had finally triumphed when, through the buffeting wind and driving rain, Abe Ryan, in a fork of steel-blue lightning, caught a half-sight of a ragbag scatter of buildings. They were doing their best to keep a hold on the ground they stood on, and not be picked up and tossed away like the debris they were. Another fork of lightning confirmed that his eyes had not conjured up his hopes, only cruelly to deceive him by dashing them again. Spent, the mare stumbled, and Ryan barely kept her from going down.

'Not far now, gal,' he coaxed the horse. His cooing words encouraged the mare to one last effort.

Just on the edge of the shack town, the mare finally gave up the ghost and folded, which left Abe Ryan with the biggest problem he had yet to contend with. A man without a horse in the desert, was a man waiting to die.

CHAPTER TEN

Abe Ryan unbuckled his saddle, slung it on to shoulders that wanted to shirk the load as soon as they experienced it, and walked the short distance to the mess of hovels that stood for a town in the hostile environment of the desert, where only men who shied away from civilization and decent folk, and the men who came after them to take them back to be punished for their misdeeds, were to be found. Ryan pocketed the badge that identified him as a seeker rather than a hider. It seemed a lifeless place, but Ryan reckoned that the lack of presence was probably down to a stranger's arrival. No one would show until it was decided whether the incomer should be welcomed or killed.

Abe Ryan's hope was that he would pass as one of a kind for long enough to get a pointer to Hannigan's Reach.

Being a lawman, he had the advantage of the

knowledge gleaned from dodgers; knowledge which could open a door, but that door would be open for a short time only. The slightest slip, and he was a dead man.

The Bewley lawman was in no doubt about the magnitude of the task ahead. The men he'd be gabbing with were men who lived by their instincts and wits, and would not be fooled for long, if at all, he thought glumly. And were he to be rumbled, his final resting place would be the hellish hole he was now entering.

His steps faltered on seeing a lanky specimen step on to the boardwalk from the saloon; a lanky specimen that had an air or familiarity. Even from a goodly distance, Abe Ryan could feel the bore of the man's eyes. As he drew nearer to him the reason for his sense of familiarity came to him. He'd seen the face before on the dodger of a black-hearted villain called Jack Salk. The recognition came as a surprise, because the last he'd heard of Salk was that he'd caught lead in a one-nag town along the border, robbing a nickel-and-dime bank. The law had given up hunting Salk, but the law had obviously been fooled by the story about his demise; a yarn probably spun by Salk himself.

Jack and Bob Salk were two brothers, but as different as they come. Jack had taken to outlawry at the tender age of fifteen when he'd shot a man, folk said, just to see how it felt to watch a man die. Bob Salk had followed a different path, becoming an odd mixture of preacher and bounty hunter. Folk who spoke of him told of a man who delivered God's redemption in one hand, and dispatched those undeserving of saving (by the Reverend Salk's judgement, not God's) by way of a lightning-fast draw.

'Howdy,' Ryan hailed cheerily, hoping that the falter in his step had not been noticed by Jack Salk who, by reputation, was not a man slow to act when things were not even remotely what he figured they should be.

It would not take much for suspicions about a man's credentials to be raised in a place where every stranger might be the man looking for you. The watcher did not return Ryan's greeting. Not good, he thought. Salk went back inside the saloon, coming back outside a moment later accompanied by another man. This time, readied, the marshal's step did not falter.

He strode confidently forward, hoping that he was a good enough actor to fool the hardcases he'd be facing any second now.

'Howdy, fellas,' he hailed again. 'Thought I wouldn't make it. My hoss buckled just at the edge of town.'

Salk still remained silent, watching, waiting like a cat ready to pounce on a mouse the second the mouse thought he'd not been noticed. The second man, smaller and beefier, returned Ryan's greeting in an equally friendly manner.

'The desert is surely a hard mistress, mister.'

Salk moved to a more central position on the boardwalk, his scrutiny of Abe Ryan even keener than it had been.

'Where do you hail from, friend?' the speaker of the pair enquired of Ryan.

'All parts,' was Ryan's answer.

'That's a lot of territory,' the spokesman replied, his manner less friendly. 'Me and Jack would like you to narrow it down some. Ain't that so, Jack?'

Salk did not need to respond verbally, his eyes spoke for him.

The searching Ryan's brain had been doing put a name to the speaker. He'd put on beef, but behind the fatter face, around the mean, black-pebble eyes, the man's identity was revealed – Ryan was parleying with Ned Ruby, a critter as mean and deadly as they came. Though still keeping up his pretence of bonhomie, Ryan noted that Ruby had placed his hands on his hips, the way a man might when innocently settling down to gab. However, the Bewley marshal had no doubt that Ruby's gesture was not one of carefree ease, but rather one of readiness. His hands were now close to resting on the Colts of the double rig he wore; guns which, by repute, could clear leather faster than the eye could see.

Pinned down by Ruby, Abe Ryan had a sense of the plan he'd arrived with (to present himself as a man of kinship with the men who frequented the shack town and Hannigan's Reach) drifting away. With no other viable plan presenting itself, he was beginning to figure that he'd bitten off yards more than he could chew, when Jack Salk threw him a lifeline.

'Ain't polite to delay a man looking to slake his thirst, Ned,' Salk said. 'Talking can follow when he rids his craw of desert dust. Why don't we step into the saloon, gents?'

Ned Ruby was clearly annoyed by Salk's intervention. For a breath-holding second he might have disagreed before agreeing, Ryan reckoned.

Ryan did not understand why Salk had thrown the lifeline, but he grabbed it. Time enough to try and figure out Salk's reason for doing so (and he figured there was a reason other than charity), between that very minute and the time it would take to have the drink Salk suggested. It would only be minutes, and he could only hope that a way out of his predicament would present itself.

On entering the ramshackle saloon, closer to a

privy than a thirst-slaking establishment, Ryan saw
that the only other customers were four men who
were playing poker at a table strategically placed in
a nook behind the batwings to give them time to
respond to any threat coming through the doors.
They paused, looked, and decided that if the
stranger had passed muster with Ruby and Salk he
was no threat to them. They turned their attention
again to card playing.

'Moonshine OK?' Salk enquired of Ryan.

'Fine with me,' the Bewley lawman replied in
the manner of a man easy with his surroundings
and the company he was keeping.

Ned Ruby chuckled. 'Good. 'Cause all we've got
'round here is moonshine brewed up in
Hannigan's Reach.'

Just in the nick of time, Abe Ryan stopped
himself from stepping into the trap he was certain
Ruby had set. And that was for Ryan to prove his
lack of credibility by asking about Hannigan's
Reach, and by so doing reveal himself as an interloper. Because any man of the kind who had
knowledge of the shack town and its transient pop-
ulation, would also know about the outlaw roost
called Hannigan's Reach. That he did not ask the
question Ruby had expected he might ask, set well
with the hardcase and the other men. Before he
knew it, the poker players had quit the game and

had bellied up to the bar, giving Ryan the breathing time he needed to come up with a plan that would gain all round credence. He had gained Ruby's confidence. However, exchanging glances with Salk, who was standing a way off from the main party, the Bewley marshal knew that he had a long way to go to satisfy Jack Salk. Salk's amused lopsided grin told him as much.

'Guess I'll take me some shut-eye,' Salk said, leaving the sorry excuse for a saloon as soon as he'd spoken. 'Be seein' you, friend,' was his parting shot to Abe Ryan, who knew that what sounded like a perfectly innocent parting to the others, was Salk's coded way of telling him that he had not fooled him one iota.

There was nothing Abe Ryan could do about it. Time alone would reveal Jack Salk's reason for not rumbling him. So, over the next minutes he cleverly manipulated the knowledge about outlawry and outlaws that he had gleaned as a lawman to ingratiate himself with the hardcase company he was supping with, craftily convincing his drinking partners of his ranking in outlawry by making himself part of the stories he had heard, while praying that none of the men present had themselves been part of those escapades. Careful to measure his consumption of moonshine on a three- or four-to-one basis, his tall tales became more and more acceptable to his increasingly ine-briated company.

Feeling the time was right, Ryan bowed out.

'You'll find fresh straw in the livery,' Ned Ruby told him, a comradely arm round his shoulders, his eyes rolling wildly with the effect of moonshine that was rawer than most potions Ryan had drunk. 'Watch for the white-faced stallion. He's a mean one. Kick you right over the moon, given half a chance.'

'Thanks for the friendly word of advice,' Ryan said.

'What're pals for, Jake,' Ruby said drunkenly, 'if not to set a fella straight?'

Jake Crowe was the name of the killing bastard, whose monicker Ryan had adopted to gain accep-tance. He had gambled on Crowe, a Missourian, not having visited these parts. It had turned out so.

'Thought I'd make myself scarce for a spell,' Ryan had said, when Ruby had enquired as to why Crowe had come to visit now. 'More lawdogs looking for me than a mangy dog's got fleas.' The joke had gone down well.

'Guess every man here's got that feeling, Jake,' Ruby said.

Feeling his confidence at a peak, the Bewley lawman decided to push his luck one measure further. 'Heard a passel of guff about this

Hannigan fella and the roost he runs round these parts. Thought I'd pay a visit and rest up for a spell.' The chatter dried up, and a pall of silence settled. Ryan knew that to let the subject drop now would only heighten the tension which had replaced the cheer. The only choice he had was to finish what he'd started for good or bad. 'Thought I might sample Hannigan's hospitality. But not being from this neck of the woods, I don't know how to find the Reach. Thought I'd get a pointer from you fellas.'

No one answered.

Time dragged.

'About five miles due east.' All eyes were on Jack Salk in the batwings. 'You'll come to a narrow canyon. A ways on, it opens out some, and shortly after you'll see a hole in the rockface that looks like the opening to a cave, but in fact is the entrance to Hannigan's Reach. Once through the entrance a steep trail takes you right to Hannigan's front door. Every inch of the trail is covered by lookouts, perched high. Any doubt on their part, like maybe if they thought that you were a slick clever lawman, they'll cut you down for sure.'

'And so they should,' Ryan barked, seemingly none too pleased with Jack Salk butting in.

Salk looked for a long time at Ryan, who knew

that if Salk gave the nod he'd be OK. However, if Salk did not give that nod, in the next minute, the Bewley marshal knew that he'd be wormbait.

'Hannigan ain't goin' to like a stranger bein' pointed towards the roost, Jack,' Ned Ruby grumbled. 'I sure hope that you're goin' to tell him it was you who did the tellin', if he asks. Hannigan can be a tetchy customer.'

There was a mumble of agreement with Ruby's assessment of the roost's keeper.

'You've got nothing to fret about, Ned,' Salk said. 'Neither has any man here. If Hannigan asks, I'll own up. But I'm sure that Hannigan won't have any problem with a visit from Jake Crowe. The meaner they come, the more welcome Hannigan makes them.'

The relief in the saloon was immense, and the crackle went out of the air.

'I think we should fill 'em up again,' one of the men said, making it first to the bar.

'You fellas be my guest,' Ryan said, putting money on the bar to keep the moonshine flowing. 'I'm bushed.'

'Only one problem left for you, Crowe,' Salk said. 'Without a horse, you'll have a real problem making it to the roost.' Abe Ryan had a feeling of Salk playing with him; of doling out rope for him to hang himself with. However, just when he'd decided that Salk was about to throw him to the wolves, his next words turned the tables again. 'Take my horse, friend.'

Jack Salk's offer stunned his cohorts. No man in his right senses would offer another man his horse, and not at all in desert country, where a nag was the difference between life and death.

'A very generous offer,' Abe Ryan said cautiously, his head spinning, trying to figure out the game Jack Salk was playing. 'But either you're the most decent *hombre* I've ever crossed paths with, Salk. Or you're as loco as they come.'

'Ned . . .' Ruby, obviously struggling to make sense of what was going on, turned to Salk. 'I'll throw my saddle on that fine specimen of horse-flesh in the livery, the stallion. Or one of the string of those other equally fine horses you and . . .' Salk looked at the man who had been first up to the bar to resume supping, 'Benny rode in with yesterday.'

Abe Ryan reckoned that he had found Mame Benteen's remuda, and Mame Benteen's killers all in the one place.

'And what're ya goin' to use for money, Salk?' Ruby snorted. 'That horse will cost you plenty.'

'That's sure a good question,' said Ruby's partner in horse-thieving, rape and murder.

Jack Salk grinned a grin that would put legs under Satan.

'Well, I kind of figured that what's not yours to begin with, you fellas wouldn't mind parting with.'

'The hell, Salk!' the man called Benny barked.

Jack Salk's prowess with an iron was legend, but there was no understanding that legend without seeing the heart-stopping speed of Salk's draw. The man who had protested so vehemently a moment before was now cringing under the threat of Salk's .45, his own pistol only half-out of leather. Looking death in the face, Benny's spunk drained away.

'I figure we can spare the stallion, don't you, Ned?' he said, pleading in his voice. He laughed jerkily as Ned Ruby remained implacable. 'Like Jack says, easy come easy go, huh?'

Jack Salk holstered his sixgun and faced Ned Ruby, unflinching and unconcerned, while Ruby weighed up his options. Salk was fast. Ruby was fast. And the only question to be answered was, which was that smidgen faster.

Benny dared not blink an eye. The stand-off between two fast draws put him in the unenviable position of having to take a fifty-fifty gamble. When Ruby, unsure, opted for fake friendliness, the weakness of relief had Benny seeking the support of the bar before his legs should buckle.

'I guess it's like Benny says, Jack,' he said, putting on a show of nonchalance. 'Easy come, easy go.'

'That's good, Ned,' Salk said. 'But I've got money to pay with.'

'You have?' Benny gulped.

'I wouldn't hold friends like Ned and you to ransom, Benny.'

'Then why all this hullabaloo?'

The question was Ned Ruby's. And it was obvious that he could not have stopped himself asking it in his usual crotchety manner, no matter what.

Salk, his voice as hard as steel, said, 'Just wanted to see if you'd finally work up the mettle to draw that iron you've been bursting to draw since I rode in three days ago, Ruby. Reckon that right now, like at any time during those days, you couldn't make up your mind which of us was faster.' Ned Ruby became stiffer than a corpse. The air was crackling again. The man called Benny went paler than new milk. The neutrals were quietly moving aside out of the line of expected gunfire, every man now suddenly as sober as the proverbial judge. 'Well, maybe some day we'll find out.' He turned to Abe Ryan. 'Let's make tracks for the livery, Jake.'

Abe Ryan had not the faintest idea of what game Salk was playing, but he figured that there was no point in speculating. Salk would make it clear only in his own good time, whenever that might be.

Going through the batwings, Salk spun, shoving Ryan aside as he did so. His gun appeared in his hand as if by sorcery. Ned Ruby's gun was just clearing leather. Only seconds made the difference between the two men. 'Ain't polite to shoot a man in the back, Ruby,' Salk growled. By the unwritten law of the West, with Ruby's treachery exposed Jack Salk was within his rights to kill him. Instead, he slid his six-gun back in its holster. 'Now that you know who's faster, Ruby, don't draw iron on me again!' He stalked out of the saloon. 'I hate it when I can read a man as easily as that. No fun at all, *Jake.*'

Jack Salk smiled, knowing well that Abe Ryan had heard his emphasis on the fictitious name in a way the others had not.

Salk knew of his charade.

So what next?

CHAPTER ELEVEN

Making their way to the livery, neither man spoke. Just when Ryan was pondering on when Jack Salk would show the best hand in the deck he held, the outlaw offered him a option. 'Do you want to explain why you're masquerading as a deadman? Or should I do that first, you reckon?'

Abe Ryan paused and stood back a couple of paces from the outlaw, puzzled and curious in equal measure.

'Yeah. Twin brothers, me and Jack,' Bob Salk said, understanding Ryan's study of him. 'Identical before this.' Bob Salk ran a piano player's finger along the deep ridge in his left cheek, which gave it a lopsided slant when compared to the right side of his face. It explained Ryan's feeling of familiarity when he had first set eyes on Bob Salk, and mistaken him for his brother Jack. He had seen a stack of dodgers for all kinds of mayhem with his brother Jack's mug on them, a replica of Bob's. 'The Brazos Kid. Played dead when he caught my lead, but he was only half dead. When I bent a knee to pray over him, he shot me with a derringer he had rigged in a spring mechanism up his sleeve, which he used if his sleight-of-hand antics in a card game were rumbled. Killed fifteen men with that lady gun. Killed double that with a pair of Colts that had smoke drifting from their barrels more often than not. Often partnered my brother Jack in mayhem.'

The Reverend Bob Salk became pensive.

'I've often pondered on how come two brothers, out of the same womb, could be so darn different. One a killer outlaw. And one a man hunter and saver of souls.'

Having paid over bounty to hunters, and having formed the opinion that they were little if no better than the men they hunted, Abe Ryan did not rate them as any better. Many times he had expressed this view. However, he was wise enough to know that there were times, like now, when an opinion was best kept to oneself.

'Kind of strange, wouldn't you say, lawman?'

Lawman?

'Before I stepped out of the saloon, curious

127

about a stranger, as a wise man would be in these parts, you raised your hand, like so,' Bob Salk gave a graphic description of Ryan's hand going to his vest pocket, sliding upwards, and then down to his trousers pocket. Exactly how it was when he had removed his marshal's badge. 'Now the question is, what are you doing here? And,' Bob Salk looked beyond Ryan, 'best to step inside the livery before you answer.' Abe Ryan looked over his shoulder. Ned Ruby and his cohorts were watching through the saloon window. 'By now I figure that, slow-witted as they are, they're beginning to think about what's going on between you and me.'

They stepped inside the ramshackle livery.

'I'm running Frank Cuskin to ground, Reverend,' Ryan said.

'Less of the Reverend. Walls have ears. Frank Cuskin, you say. The devil himself. Deserves to be hunted down.' Bob Salk studied Abe Ryan. 'Won't be easy bringing Cuskin to book.'

Ryan's smile was a wry one. 'That's not new information, sir.' The Bewley marshal shared with Salk the story of him and Cuskin so far.

'Maybe you should count your blessings and cut your losses. I figure that the next time Cuskin catches sight of you he'll make sure that when he puts you down, you'll stay down. If you like, I might be able to fit Cuskin in to my busy schedule,' Salk offered.

'Forget it, Salk,' Ryan said sternly. 'Frank Cuskin goes back to Bewley with me to hang for murder.'

'An admirable ambition.' Bob Salk snorted derisively, obviously of the opinion that Ryan was ill-equipped to accomplish what he had set out to do. 'Even if you nail Cuskin . . . *again,* there's his two brothers and whole passel of cut-throats he can call on.'

'I'll take my chances,' Ryan said grimly. The way I see it, it's Cuskin or me. Plain and simple.'

'I wish you well. Now I reckon that the stallion would be better than my nag to get you to Hannigan's Reach.'

'That's a very generous gesture,' Ryan said.

'Don't be so quick to thank me. I'm probably sending you to your death.'

'What are you doing here, Reverend? Don't reckon there's a pulpit here.'

'I got word that Larry and Ben Egan are headed this way to the border. I figure that this dead-end hole will likely be on their visiting list. Once they drop in, well. . . .' Bob Salk shrugged. 'I reckon those boys will be staying around permanently.'

Aware of Salk's reputation as a bounty hunter, Abe Ryan reckoned the same way.

'How do you figure on getting Cuskin out of the

Reach? That's if you get in to start with,' Salk added darkly.

Ryan shrugged philosophically. 'I reckon the way will be pointed out.'

'I admire a man with faith, sir. I wish you luck, friend.'

'Thanks. I reckon I'm going to need a whole pile of that.'

Bob Salk nodded in agreement.

'Want me to say a blessing over you before you leave?'

'Can't do any harm.' Abe Ryan studied Bob Salk curiously, a man he'd grown to like in their short acquaintance. He did not understand the mix that made Salk what he was. He didn't approve or disapprove. But he reckoned that when taken as a whole, there was probably more good than bad in Bob Salk.

Boots sounded on the boardwalk.

'Best be making tracks,' Salk advised Ryan. 'Out the back way. The front might have lead in the air.'

'Will you be OK?' Ryan was genuinely concerned.

'Sure,' Salk said confidently. 'Ruby's standing with his cohorts will be way down. And I figure that no man will want to try me, having witnessed my prowess with a shooting iron.'

'Figure not.'

'A last word of advice. When you get near to the canyon leading to the Reach, swing south for a spell. You'll come to a pass that enters the canyon further along. It'll bring you out behind the look-outs.'

'Thanks.'

'Don't thank me, friend. This pass is little more than a crack in the rock. Barely horsewide, and a shade for snakes.'

'How will I know when to swing south?'

'You'll come to outcrops of rock, like sentries guarding the canyon ahead. Begin your swing at the seventh outcrop. Now bow your head for that blessing, and pray the Lord's Prayer.'

'Ain't too sure about the words,' Ryan said.

'You're a heathen, aren't you?' the Reverend Bob Salk pronounced, the hellfire of the pulpit in his eyes. 'Well,' he said despondently, 'say what you can of them and mumble in between. Maybe the Lord God won't be listening too closely. And if he is, he'll be of a mind to turn a deaf ear.

'You know, maybe you'll get Cuskin out of the Reach at that. Going right into that nest of vipers is such a loco idea, it might just work. Because no one will be expecting any man to be that crazy.'

Blessing done with, Marshal Abe Ryan high-tailed it, leaving behind one of the strangest meetings he had ever attended, and one of the strangest men he had ever met: the Reverend Bob Salk, part demon, part saint.

CHAPTER TWELVE

The stallion was as eager to eat trail as the marshal was, but Abe Ryan knew that a fast-moving rider always attracted attention, and in bandit country within a day's ride of the border, all the more. He'd have wished that the flat country he was traversing was not as bare of cover as it was, but with an outlaw roost in the neighbourhood, he wouldn't have expected anything else. The men who guested in Hannigan's Reach needed to have a clear sight of the surrounding country to give timely warning of possible trouble in the shape of the law, to either mount a challenge if the approaching law was thin on the ground, or to hightail it if it was a sizeable posse.

Other than the outlaw trash in Hannigan's Reach, Abe Ryan had Indians to worry about. Maybe the Apaches he'd dispatched might not be found for days, or not at all. But if discovered, the Apaches would be looking to avenge them. Another risk was that Ned Ruby and his cohorts, sober, might begin to see the cracks in the tall tales he'd spun them and, riled that they'd been suckered, decide to follow him to gain satisfaction, or to alert those in the roost about an interloper of suspect credentials heading their way.

As the day drew on into evening, trouble free, Abe Ryan began to think that after all his luck might be in. Coming on a series of outcrops of rock, as Bob Salk had described, each outcrop a little higher and more formidable than the previous one, Ryan figured that he had encountered what the reverend had termed the sentries for the canyon that led to Hannigan's Reach. Counting off, at the seventh outcrop he did as Salk advised and made his swing.

He was riding for a longish spell, and beginning to fret that he'd missed the pass into the canyon of which Salk had spoken when, about to back-track, he saw what looked like nothing more than a crack in a rockface that curved upwards like the humped back of an old man sitting. Horsewide was how Bob Salk had described the pass, and horsewide it was. It stank, was dark, airless, and eerily uninviting. Salk's warning about the pass being a shade for snakes raised Abe Ryan's anxiety. However, if

Cuskin was to keep an appointment with a noose in Bewley, negotiating the narrow and dangerous pass made the chance of that happening, (if Salk was right when he said that he'd come out in the canyon behind the lookouts) more likely.

Once inside, Ryan's only guide to the pass's exit was a pencil-wide strip of light that seemed a long way off. In fact, unreachable.

Abe Ryan felt his throat go dry and his pulse race.

There was a dank, sweet scent in the passage that clawed away his breath. A man born to open spaces, he fought back the panic which was creeping up on him and threatening to overwhelm him. The stallion, too, was sharing in his feeling of live burial. He thought about backing up, but even if he'd wanted to, the stallion was too frightened to be cooperative.

The pass narrowed even further.

Ryan heard the hiss of snakes!

He struggled to hold on to the stallion, his eyes fixed doggedly on the strip of light ahead which was widening. Or was he fooling himself with false hope? The walls of the pass seemed to close in on him, relentlessly determined to crush him. Ryan knew that the shortage of oxygen was a factor in causing the illusion, but reason now blurred would soon vanish altogether. Something clattered at his feet. He looked down.

Bones.

The pass had claimed at least one victim, but he had no doubt that there were other men's bones forming the dust of the pass. His, he was sure, would be there for some other fool to find.

Abe Ryan was ready to give in when the strip of light became a shaft. Hope renewed, he struggled forward. The edges of a fresh breeze refreshed him.

Just a little more. . . .

Just a little more still. . . .

One last push. . . .

Sunlight!

Fresh air.

Peace of mind.

Abe Ryan lay on the ground, sucking great gulps of air into lungs that were on fire. Calm was not in a hurry to take hold of him, and panic left him only slowly. When his strength returned, he sat up and looked round him.

He was, as Salk had said he would be, deeper into the canyon. He looked back along and saw that Salk had been right. Two men were perched high up, looking the other way, never figuring on anyone being behind them. He wasn't sure if he should pray for or curse Bob Salk. Not alone had he found his way into Hannigan's Reach. But he reckoned that the way in would also be his way out with Cuskin.

Maybe, after all, he would succeed in taking Cuskin back to Bewley.

Maybe.

CHAPTER THIRTEEN

There it was, Hannigan's Reach. A saucer-shaped, fertile valley, where no one would expect a valley to be. Horses roamed contentedly free on the lush pasture, nourished by a waterfall which bubbled up from deep inside the rock. It filled a reservoir, the water from which was distributed by a series of dykes to the pasture. The valley, in an otherwise hostile environment, was a piece of heaven which must have dropped from the sky. Abe Ryan thought it odd that such a heavenly setting should be a refuge for men who were far removed by their deeds from good.

A string of cabins stretched along the edge of the valley in a half-moon. A bigger structure was lying back against a rockface. The man staggering

138

out with a woman on his arm, dressed in the sort of finery that would adorn a dove in any town saloon, identified the structure's type and purpose, even without the tinkling piano music drifting from it to float on the eddies of sweet air blowing off the high walls of the Reach. At the far end of the valley, away from its more rowdy centre, a large-bellied man sat on a rocker on the porch of a mighty fine house, the match of any gentleman's residence in Bewley or any other town.

Hannigan, Ryan guessed.

He let the stallion amble down the trail into the Reach. The scent of mares made the stallion want to make haste, but Ryan held him on a tight rein. His approach had to be measured and unhurried, not bringing undue attention to him. The residents of the roost would take it for granted that, seeing an incomer at this point, he would have been checked out and OK'd by the lookouts, though it worried him some that the giant of a man, who he had assumed was Hannigan, had stood up and come to the front of the porch to watch. It worried him even more when Hannigan went inside the house and came back out with a powerful spyglass. Curiosity? Or suspicion?

Ryan veered towards the saloon, at an angle that offered his back to Hannigan. He hoped the move had appeared casual and natural. But if Hannigan had not accepted his change of direction as he'd hoped, the roost owner would quickly cotton on to what Ryan had done, when the direct route to the saloon would have taken him there faster. Ryan made a pretence of checking out his surroundings, as a reason for his change of direction.

There was nothing he could do, but wait for the outcome.

'*Señor*!'

Ryan turned slowly from the saloon hitch rail, unsure of what the hail meant. Being close to the border, it would be no surprise to find Mexican *bandidos* and American outlaws sharing the refuge, as their crimes straddled both sides of the Rio Grande, and would have American and Mexican law seeking them out.

The Mexican was unarmed except for a Bowie tucked in a scarlet sash waistband.

'Howdy,' Ryan greeted the Mexican affably.

The Mexican's study of him was at first fleeting, but became more intense as the seconds ticked away.

'*Señor*, the rules,' he said.

Rules. What rules?

Obviously there were protocols which the outlaw fraternity would be aware of. Abe Ryan had another hurdle to get over. It would be one of many, any one of which could unmask him. He could only bluff, and hope that the Mexican would guide him. He chuckled lazily. 'I say somesing funny?' the Mexican asked abrasively. Rumbled now, and he'd probably be hauled to the top of the canyon and pitched off.

'Yeah,' Ryan drawled. 'The rules.'

Worryingly, the Mexican did not offer the enlightenment he had hoped for. He had come through hell to take Frank Cuskin back to Bewley, and now it looked as if Cuskin would have the last laugh.

'No gettin' out of it, friend.'

Ryan glanced at an unshaven, bleary-eyed man (whom he recognized from a dodger but could not now put a name to) who had staggered from the saloon.

Ryan laughed. 'Guess not, huh. Can't blame a man for trying, though.'

'Tryin' could have Hannigan skin you alive, mister,' confided the Mexican. 'Don't like no one to diddle him out of a stinkin' dime.'

Abe Ryan breathed a little more easily, but not much. The Mexican, who now had his hand out, was looking for some kind of dues. But how much?

He had been fortunate that the man, halfway to being skunk-drunk, was at the garrulous stage of inebriation and ready to take on all comers, especially those whom he saw as fleecing him, a category of man which Hannigan was obviously perceived to be.

'Ten dollars,' the man slapped a hand on the saloon hitch rail. 'Hitch fee, Hannigan calls it.'

'Meester Hannigan,' the Mexican said.

Abe Ryan breathed a whole lot easier.

'Shut your mouth, ya stinkin' Mex,' roared the man who had come out from the saloon. 'Ya know, I figure that Hannigan's got it worked out right. Sitting up in his fine big house, collectin' dollars faster than I can rob them from banks,' he groused. 'Ten dollars to hitch your horse. Another ten to sit at a table in the saloon. Two dollars for a one-shot moonshine. Twenty dollars for a cabin.'

He shook his head, his face suffused with anger; he was long past caring if what he said was overheard and caused umbrage.

'Fifteen dollars to sleep in the livery. Two dollars for a one-shot whiskey. And thirty dollars for a woman.'

Ryan had a complete tariff, knowledge of which might get him out of a tight spot later.

'Hannigan says that if he charged any less, fellas would hang around too long, and stop other fellas from using the roost,' the drunk grumbled. 'His excuse for skinnin' a man of every dime he's got!'

'I guess Hannigan has a point,' Ryan said, grateful to the drunk for his unsuspecting help. But now he needed to prevent any idea getting around that he was of the same opinion, and find himself kicked out of the Reach.

'That a fact?' the man growled. 'That's what's wrong round here. Everyone licks Hannigan's rear end!'

A hawk-faced man appeared from the side of the saloon. 'Is that so, Burke?'

Burke. Now Ryan could match name and face. Daniel Alfred Burke, the subject of many dodgers: Hawk-face had to be very fast with a gun, or very dull in the head, to chastise a killer of Burke's polecat calibre.

'I reckon you owe Mr Hannigan an apology, Burke,' Hawk-face said.

'Ya do, do ya?' Burke snorted. 'I happen to think I don't. Now,' Burke spread his legs, his hand in a claw over his Colt .45. 'You goin' to make me say sorry, pretty please? Huh?'

'Stand easy, Ben.' Everyone spun around on hearing Hannigan's deep mellifluous voice. 'I'm sure that Mr Burke is just liquored up and letting off steam.' A second gunnie put in an appearance. 'Ain't that so?'

Realizing the knife-edge he was on, Burke paled. His tongue licked suddenly dry lips. The spectre of the Grim Reaper haunted his eyes.

'Sure, Mr Hannigan,' he said, his mouth stuffed

chock-full of humble pie. 'Sure sorry if I gave any offence.'

'I know you are,' Hannigan said generously, and winked at his hirelings.

A hail of lead tossed Burke back inside the saloon, like a castaway rag doll.

'Howdy,' Hannigan greeted Abe Ryan. 'Mighty nice to see you. If I knew your monicker, I could call you by it,' he added.

Abe Ryan held out his hand to shake.

'Jake Crowe, sir.'

Ryan knew that he had now taken the biggest gamble yet. Hannigan would have undoubtedly heard of the notorious killer and bank robber, but had he ever come face to face with him? If he had not, would anyone in the roost know Crowe?. This was not Crowe territory, but he might have visited. Any outlaw in the roost might have done business in his neck of the woods.

As he sized up Ryan, Hannigan was giving nothing away. But Ryan felt an icy finger run along his spine.

CHAPTER FOURTEEN

'A ways out of your territory, ain't you, Crowe?' Hanningan said eventually, having studied Ryan. Was the roost owner making conversation or setting a trap?

Ryan shrugged and chuckled. 'Sometimes it's healthier to go where the heat is less, sir.'

'We ain't easy to find.'

It was time to gamble again, and Ryan wondered how many times he could push his luck. It had to be near its limit.

'Ned Ruby pointed the way,' he said.

'Ruby, huh?' Hannigan snorted. 'Must say that you could have arrived with a better reference. Ruby's nothing but trouble with a capital T.'

'Ned can be a tetchy *hombre* when the humour takes him,' Ryan agreed. 'Does this mean I ain't welcome?'

145

'If you've got dollars to spend, that makes you welcome,' Hannigan said.

'I've got dollars, sir,' boasted the Bewley lawman, conscious of the small change that would be left in his pocket when he'd paid the hitching dues.

'Hungry?'

'More thirsty,' Ryan said, fearing that if a one shot-glass of moonshine cost two dollars, grub would be a whole lot more of what he had not got.

'Belly up to the bar then,' Hannigan said. He shouted: 'Yang!'

A Chinese man came shuffling from behind the saloon. 'Yes siree, Misteree Hannigan.'

'There's some trash in the saloon needs tending to.'

'Yes, Misteree Hannigan.'

'That'll be *Mister* Hannigan! How many times must I tell you!' Hannigan's fist shot out to send the Chinaman reeling backwards.

'Yes, sireee,' Yang grovelled, picking himself up unsurprised; obviously he'd been the recipient of Hannigan's bad temper on many previous occasions. He bowed and hurried away.

Hannigan's laughter was harshly cruel.

'Wouldn't you wish that Americans were as polite?'

'Sure would,' Ryan agreed, his snide laughter of

camaraderie earning him, he hoped, Hannigan's approval, when in fact he would have liked to knock the roost owner on his backside.

Hannigan's laughter ceased abruptly.

'Make any trouble, or default on your bills, Crowe.' He nodded in his hardcases' direction. 'Ben and Art will be upset. You wouldn't want that. They're real mean bastards. Ain't that so, fellas.'

'Sure is, Mr Hannigan,' Ben and Art sang out.

'I ain't planning on being trouble,' Ryan said.

'Then you'll find Hannigan's Reach suits you. And Hannigan a sociable cuss.'

Hannigan turned away and strode off.

Art stepped forward.

'I don't like you, friend. So don't give me no opportunity to vent my feelings.'

Ryan snarled, 'I don't give a damn whether you like me or not.' He pushed the man aside and strode towards the saloon, feeling that his reaction had been measured, and had been what had been expected. He paused for the briefest time, apparently to appraise Hannigan's enforcers, before pushing on into the saloon. But the real purpose of his perusal was to try and get a hint as to where Cuskin might be; that was, of course, he thought darkly, if he was not in the saloon watching. Waiting like a spider in his web.

The Bewley marshal swallowed hard. Entering

the saloon, he was the subject of immediate and intense scrutiny. He half-expected a shout from Cuskin, and he let his hand hover close to his six-gun; not that drawing it would do much good. Any gunfire from him would be answered by a hail of hot lead. The best he could expect, if that shout came, was to nail Cuskin before he himself was nailed.

He slapped two dollars on to the bar. The barkeep spat into a one-shot. 'They get dusty,' he explained. He placed the one-shot in front of Ryan and poured. 'Best keep your ass tight when that hits the spot,' he advised. 'If the batch is a tad off, it can be like a steam train going through you.'

'Obliged,' Ryan said, his apprehension easing, figuring that if Cuskin was in the saloon trouble would have come a-calling before now. He turned brazenly to face his scrutineers. He raised his glass in salute. 'The name's Jake Crowe.' Abe Ryan held his breath, but on his uttering of the name of the notorious outlaw legend he was posing as, his acceptance by those in the saloon was immediate and unstinting. Men crowded up to the bar, vying with each other to buy liquor for Ryan. Wisely, the marshal excused himself, claiming that he'd been riding flat out for days and needed shuteye. Every man there understood, because every man there had been through the ordeal of hard riding and bullet-dodging.

Now he was left with only one problem, and that was to find out where Frank Cuskin was, at the same time hoping that he had not skipped the Reach and headed straight for Mexico.

'Straw or cabin?' enquired the barkeep.

'Neither, barkeep,' Ryan said, keenly aware of the little he had in his pocket. 'With posses hounding me most times, I've gotten kind of partial to having the wind on my face when I sleep. So I'll just pick me a spot and curl up, if that's OK with you?'

It was obviously a new situation and the barkeep was at a loss.

'OK by me,' he finally said. 'But I'll have to report to Mr Hannigan. We ain't got no charge for what you want to do.'

'If Mr Hannigan feels that I should pay, barkeep, then I'll darn well cough up.'

Easier of mind, the barkeep said, 'Enjoy your shuteye, Mr Crowe.'

'Surely will. See you fellas later.' Ryan waved cheerily as he took his leave.

Passing the window of the saloon, a shimmer of something caught his eye. Alarm bells rang loud and clear. He knew what was glistening before he checked. His marshal's badge was hanging by its clasp to the edge of his pants pocket; the pocket from which he had taken the money with which to pay for his one-shot. He was the fool of all fools not to have rid himself of the lawman's emblem after Bob Salk had brought his attention to it. Not to have done so now put him in great danger. Had the badge been seen by one of the no-goods in the saloon? And if not, would attention be drawn to it now, reflecting the sun as it was. If its shimmer had caught his eye, then chances were that it had caught someone else's eye also. He thought about shoving the badge back into his pocket, but resisted the impulse to do so. Any movement might focus eyes on him. Ten feet or so would see him clear of the saloon window.

Marshal Abe Ryan walked on, tense, listening for the slightest sound that would alert him to a bullet in the back. Biding time became a habit with the kind of men who frequented Hannigan's Reach. It was what they spent a great deal of their time doing.

A mountain of possible problems was Ryan's lot. With many more to come, before Frank Cuskin's neck was stretched back in Bewley – if his neck *was* stretched back in Bewley.

Ahead, a furious, swearing Mexican woman stormed out of a cabin. 'Rot in hell!' she shouted back into the cabin before slamming the door shut.

'I could do without a whore having a spat with

her customer right now,' Ryan mumbled, thinking that the luck which had stayed with him for so long was about to run out, because the woman, still screaming and swearing, would turn all eyes her way and consequently his way too.

Striding past Ryan, unseeing or uncaring in her rage, she bumped into him, her ample proportions providing enough force and momentum to knock him out of his stride. 'I hate all gringos,' she berated him.

'All gringos are not the same, ma'am,' Ryan said.

'Hah!' she squealed. 'Prove it.'

'How would I do that?' Ryan queried.

'Go shoot that gringo Cuskin for me.'

Ryan held his breath. 'Cuskin?'

She pointed to the cabin she had burst from. 'The pig I lie with. You do this for me?'

'I'm sure whatever he did, wouldn't—'

'Hah! You see.' She coughed up a copious amount of phlegm and spat it out, forcing Ryan to sidestep the spittle. 'Gringos,' she said contemptuously. Though she gave full vent to her opinion of gringos in Spanish, Abe Ryan did not need to know the lingo to get the drift of her sentiments. Before she marched on he took advantage of the cover her more than ample body gave to slide the marshal's badge into his pocket.

The cabin door opened. Naked and drunk, Frank Cuskin matched the woman's vitriol. Ryan quickly turned away. It would be unlikely that, in the state the outlaw was in, he'd have taken any notice. But now that Lady Luck had favoured him, Ryan was not about to spit in her eye.

The men in the saloon had piled out to join in the hoo-ha, stirring a pot that was already boiling over. In response, Frank Cuskin cut loose with a string of bad-tempered, foul-mouthed expletives, before slamming the cabin door shut again with a vigour fit to bring the cabin down.

Responding in kind, the men returned inside the saloon, taking the Mexican whore in their charge, all ready to bed whoever.

Ryan let the dust settle, before walking cautiously to Cuskin's cabin. He paused outside the cabin door to check the neighbourhood, and he porch of Hannigan's house. All was quiet. He eased open the door and quickly stepped inside.

'Come back for more fun and games, have you, Mex?'

Ryan shot a glance into the far corner of the cabin, where Cuskin was lying in bed, his back turned to him. The Bewley lawman reached the bed in a couple of loping strides, and put the barrel of his six-gun to Frank Cuskin's head.

'Get dressed, Cuskin!'

Unable to curb his astonishment, the outlaw rolled over and looked wide-eyed at Abe Ryan, sobering instantly.

'Easy now,' the marshal warned. 'Could have got your head blown off.'

'How the—?'

'It's a long and mightily interesting story,' Ryan said. 'Maybe I'll tell you all about it on the way back to Bewley.'

Recovered from his astonishment, Cuskin snorted, 'You've got a real sense of humour, Ryan. That I'll give you. There's no way you're gettin' out of here. Except feet first!'

'Well, that makes two of us,' Ryan drawled. 'If I die, you die, Cuskin.'

Fear haunted the outlaw's eyes. The nightmare of Ryan turning up on his doorstep again had, despite his best efforts, come to pass.

'So you'd better make sure that I keep sucking air. Get dressed,' Ryan continued.

The outlaw slid out of bed. Ryan grabbed the gunbelt hanging on the back of a chair alongside the bed. He emptied the chamber of Cuskin's gun, and put the weapon back in the holster. The outlaw's gaze flitted across the full gunbelt.

'Not a chance, Cuskin,' Ryan said. 'Try and reload and I'll blow a hole in you. You wear the rig, as normal. A gunbelt without any bullets might give some curious critter food for thought.'

Frank Cuskin got dressed.

'Now, we're going to step outside, laughing and joshing like long-lost pals. Then you'll spin a yarn to get us mounted and riding, Cuskin. Or. . . .'

Abe Ryan cocked the .45.

No fool, Frank Cuskin knew that the Bewley marshal held all the aces in the deck. However, hope was not lost. He'd dealt with men who held all the aces before. This was just another inconvenience to be worked through. He slid his empty six-gun back into its holster.

'Move!' Ryan ordered.

Following on Cuskin's heels, Ryan took off his hat and covered his cocked pistol with it. The lawman knew that there would be many dangerous and deadly moments before they reached Bewley. But those that passed until they cleared the Reach would be the deadliest of all.

When they stepped outside there was no one around.

'Get your horse,' Ryan instructed.

As they passed the saloon on their way to the livery someone hailed Cuskin.

'Hey, Frank. I heard you was a real dog with that Mex woman. She's fixing to kill ya.'

'Join in the humour,' Ryan murmured. 'Then move on quickly.'

154

Cuskin laughed, and called back, 'I guess it might be worth it at that, Larry.'

'Ain't ya goin' to slake your thirst, Frank?'

'Make it good. And make it believable,' Ryan grated.

'Naw. Me and my good pal—'

'Hold it,' Ryan said urgently. 'The name's Jake Crowe.'

'—Jake got to talkin', and we figured that we'd go and empty a coupla strongboxes.'

'Good idea,' Larry agreed.

'We'll be back in a coupla days, and the drinks will be on us, Larry.'

'Look forward to that,' Larry said eagerly.

'Tell the rest of the boys.'

'Sure will. Kill a coupla lawdogs for me and the boys.'

'A dozen enough?' Cuskin joked.

'I say, the more the merrier, Frank.'

'Walk on, Cuskin,' Ryan ordered. 'Make it a real casual stroll, too.'

Marshal Abe Ryan breathed a little easier. He had almost come unstuck by not having briefed Cuskin on the alias he was using.

Mounted up, they rode across the valley at a leisurely pace, despite Ryan's urge to clip it.

'You're wastin' your time, Ryan,' Cuskin scoffed.

'You'll never get past the lookouts. Those boys have got eagle eyes.'

'How do you figure I got past them on the way in, Cuskin?'

Cuskin's eyes flashed deep concern.

'I've got a plan, Cuskin,' Ryan boasted. 'A real cute plan.'

Doubt, as heavy as a wet blanket, took hold of Cuskin. That doubt grew ever keener as they cleared the valley and headed back down the trail from the Reach to the canyon. On reaching the narrow pass through which Ryan had entered the canyon, he told Cuskin, 'This is where we leave. And be quick about it.' Ryan kept a keen eye on the lookouts' perch, praying that their concentration, as when he had entered the canyon, would remain firmly to the front.

'We'll never squeeze through there,' Cuskin complained.

'I got in, so I reckon we can get out. Just one thing: try anything and I'll blast you to hell, Cuskin.'

Ten minutes later, lathered with sweat, Cuskin and Ryan emerged from the pass.

'The lookouts will—'

'Won't even know we're around. We've come out on a blind spot. Ride, Cuskin. You're gallows bound.'

On hearing the excited babble from the street, Kate Collins rushed outside. Her heart leaped on seeing a dishevelled, thin-as-a-rake, exhausted Abe Ryan riding tail on a downcast Frank Cuskin. She had given up hope of ever setting eyes on Abe again.

'Got me some business I must finish, Kate,' Ryan hailed, passing by. 'Be calling on you presently, gal.'

The crowd that was lining the boardwalk all the way to the jail to witness the notorious Frank Cuskin being locked up scattered on seeing two men step from the livery. One of the men held a pistol to the livery owner's head. Abe Ryan had never laid eyes on Frank Cuskin's brothers, but he had no doubt about who the men were.

'Thought we'd save ourselves all that hard ridin'' to rescue Frank, Marshal,' said the older of the pair. 'Figured we'd wait 'til you arrived back in town.'

'You just let Frank ride on with us, Marshal,' said the second Cuskin. 'And there'll be no trouble.'

'Can't do that, gents,' Ryan said. 'Frank's got an appointment with the hangman.'

'Don't be dumb, Marshal. We'll kill you and,' he raised his voice, 'a whole lot more if you get stubborn.'

Kate Collins slipped back inside her store.

The crowd, that just moments before had been singing Abe Ryan's praises, now turned against him, many calling on him to do what the Cuskins demanded he do.

'Now just to show that we mean what we say, Marshal. . . .' The younger of the Cuskin demons shot the livery owner, and cast him aside like trash.

Ryan threw himself from the stallion, gun in hand. As he landed on the ground, the excited horse milled about, preventing the Cuskins from getting a clear shot at him. The marshal got one clear-cut chance and fired. The Cuskin who had murdered the livery man, grabbed his chest, wobbled, dropped to his knees, stricken, and fell face down in the street. The other Cuskin brother got off a shot that grazed the side of Ryan's head knocking him off balance, stunned. The standing Cuskin moved quickly to stand over Ryan.

'Shoot him, brother,' Frank Cuskin shouted.

'I aim to, he brother,' said Sam Cuskin. 'But you wouldn't c   little pleasure now would you.'

'Drop it!'

The Cuskins lo

Collins, who was now holding Sam Cuskin under